She was determined to catch the men who stole her fiancé but fate intervened...

The radio blared, and her teeth gritted. The past consumed her all over again. The sensation garnered steam and sliced through her like a razor blade. She whipped her head to the side around a particularly challenging turn. The gas pedal pushed itself to the floor, and her leg stiffened in the forward position. The pickup rocked. It shimmied and shook on a higher than normal center of gravity, and fields of grass rose around her. Her spirit shook, and a demon nearly broke her in half. Nothing was as it seemed, and all of her plans changed in an instant. Something was out of place. Amiss. Sensations roamed through her like a fog. Rain cascaded down on her windshield, and splattered in nickels and dimes. Big droplets. Little ones. It was all the same.

The road before her blurred in the gray and the rain. A car swerved out in front of her, as it misjudged the gap in traffic. She jerked the wheel, but not soon enough. She swerved. The car in front of her swerved, but in the same direction. The collision was profound and immediate. Crunching metal and bending glass. Shards scattered. Her dreams shattered. An explosion. The right side of her car imploded.

The impact crushed her passenger window. Her head bobbed, and the airbag exploded.

Elisha Crimson thought her wedding day would be the happiest of her life. But losing her fiancé to two thugs in a dark sedan wasn't part of the plan. She, along with the rest of the wedding party, can do nothing to stop the abrupt abduction, so she pursues at the first opportunity, navigating the West Virginia interstate in a white wedding dress behind the wheel of a pickup truck. But will she catch the sedan in time to save her one true love?

Ronnie Washington had known his past would catch up with him, eventually, but he hadn't expected it to happen on his wedding day. He hates enclosed spaces, and now he's bouncing around in the trunk of a car after being abducted from the ceremony. His only hope is to talk his way out, but the thugs don't seem inclined to listen. He knows Elisha will come after him, but, even if she catches them, what can she possibly do against men like these?

Can these two unlikely heroes save the day, and the wedding, or is their life together over before it even starts?

gives chase. But the black sedan is faster, and the men who abducted Ronnie have guns, so what will she do if she actually catches them? Spit chewing tobacco at them? She doesn't know, but she is determined to try, until tragedy strikes, and the black sedan leaves her far behind. Now it's a hunt instead of a chase, but is she still in the game? *The Bridal Chase* is clever, intriguing, and just a little corny. The characters are both charming and endearing, the action fast paced, the plot full of twists and turns. It will make you smile and chew your nails, all at the same time. *~ Regan Murphy, The Review Team of Taylor Jones & Regan Murphy*

ACKNOWLEDGMENTS

If it wasn't for a writing prompt in either *The Writer* or *Writer's Digest*, this novella never would have come into existence. I can't remember which magazine actually prompted me. Maybe it's better that way, since both magazines have been equally helpful to me over the years. NaNoWriMo 2014 with all of its statistics and graphs allowed me to complete the first draft, and now here we are. Thank you to Black Opal Books for once again taking a chance on me and this novella. Lauri and Faith and the rest of the team have been fantastic, and I can't sing their praises loud enough. Faith saw the good in it amongst the chaos. This novella is the best it can be because of you.

I owe my dad a huge debt of gratitude. He has singlehandedly built me a steady stream of readers in Fairmont, and he's called in so many favors to help me out I know he's lost count. My brother and his lovely wife as well as my mom and dad provided great feedback on my cover. My entire family who has endlessly promoted my writing and my Facebook page. My readers who ensure I don't spend all of my time talking to myself, and my fellow writers for providing tips, trade secrets, and countless rounds of encouragement. And I'd like to thank God, who always makes the impossible

possible. Any errors in judgment have, and always will be, my own.

THE BRIDAL CHASE

A Novella

ROBERT DOWNS

A Black Opal Books Publication

GENRE: MYSTERY/SUSPENSE

THE BRIDAL CHASE
Copyright © 2018 by Robert Downs
Cover Design by Jackson Cover Designs
All cover art copyright © 2018
All Rights Reserved
Print ISBN: 978-1-626949-07-2

First Publication: MAY 2018

Published by Black Opal Books **http://www.blackopalbooks.com**

DEDICATION

For my mom,
who taught me to chase after my dreams

CHAPTER 1

Saturday, 2:45 p.m.:

Her long, white dress billowed around her. Mascara raced down her face, her eyes frazzled, and a tear formed as she took off at a dead run. Her brother tossed her his set of keys. She caught them in midair and didn't even break stride. She peeled out of the parking lot, as a spray of gravel pinged a Mercedes, two BMWs, and a Lexus. Through the open window, the wind whipped her hair. Her green eyes were fixed at a distant point on the horizon. Her gaze was just a bit above the dashboard, as she slammed the pickup truck into second gear. A string of curse words emitted from her lips and smacked the wheel. The cup holder beside her held a plastic cup filled with spit, and she picked it up now. Tobacco juice flowed from her lips, and into its predetermined location.

Elisha Crimson flipped the air conditioner on high, even though it was only sixty degrees outside. She honked her horn, gestured with her free hand, and merged into the passing lane. A silver car swerved in front of her, and she screamed and pounded the steering wheel in agony. This time, she neglected to salute the idiot behind the wheel with a cell phone pressed to his ear.

Her eyes flipped to her rearview mirror, and the sea of cars behind her in an intricate rainbow of colors. The trail of cars resembled a python, and the road in front of her was a never-ending façade of red taillights. An accident loomed up ahead, so she slowed down. Two cars—neither one moving—in the right-hand lane were both torn to shreds in twisted metal and crumpled bumpers. Her mind raced, and adrenaline shook her right hand.

She grabbed the cup beside her and spit another glob of juice.

She'd nailed second gear within five hundred feet of the parking lot, and third came soon after. Fourth proved a bit more of a challenge, but now that was behind her as well. Her lips moved at a constant, steady pace, and the cup beside her filled quickly as well. The pouch stuffed between the passenger seat and her own was a third gone.

She hadn't smiled since this morning with her hairdresser and sister in the same room, as her mother waited in the room next to hers. Elisha flipped the radio low and her voice high. A rapper spoke about life in the ghetto.

She held onto the steering wheel until her knuckles turned white, and her joints ached. A song came on the radio that reminded her of him, and she turned up the volume loud enough to rattle the frame. With the windows rolled down, the sound traveled toward the trees on either side of the highway. A motorcycle engine roared behind her, and she pushed the pedal all the way to the floor. She smacked her lips and tapped her forehead. She kept thoughts—of her fiancé, her wedding, and the family she left behind—to herself and slammed down the lid. She discovered a ball cap within arm's reach and thumped it on her head.

She floored it around an old Porsche and a Mercedes with custom wheels. She held one thought and then another: What would her family think? How could this be happening to her? Was her fiancé okay?— collecting them like stamps and compartmentalizing each one in her mind until such a time when she could gather them whole and shove forward with her life.

She'd known Ronnie's past would catch up with them one day, but now was not the time for second guesses.

She kept one eye on the horizon and her goal in mind. Her whole world changed when a car pulled out in front of her. She veered to the left, the pickup nearly coming up on two wheels, the center of gravity shifting with brute force. And then she shoved the pickup hard to the right, as the center of gravity changed once again, and the whole cab moved and shook around her. The wind whipped through with blazing speed, and her knuckles locked against the wheel. She pinged to the right and careened to the left like a ping pong ball through a maze.

Steam rose up around her, and she hoped it wasn't her own. She bit her lip and drew blood, and even managed to swallow a little of the chewing tobacco. Coughing and gagging and sick to her stomach, she had no idea how to continue onward. Only that she had to. If she failed, she couldn't deal with the consequences.

She had insisted on a big wedding filled with a dessert buffet, two guitars, one ice sculpture, three photographers, and one deejay. Had she scaled back, she might have found herself in a different predicament than the one she currently found herself in the middle of. The voice on the radio called her a liar.

She discovered love at eighteen when it bit her on the ass and decided to hang around. The fucker, Ronnie Washington, had smiled at her, and her knees buckled in the heat and humidity. Unable to string a coherent sentence together for five minutes, she waited for him to walk away. But he didn't. Ten minutes later, he asked her out, and she said yes before she gathered what remained of her senses. Six years later—the best six years of her life—he still asked her out, the romantic bastard. Sure, the ups and downs sucked, and he charmed her with all five of his senses, but dammit she loved him anyway. She loved him with her entire body, and still that didn't seem like enough. Now, in her brother's pickup, with her whole world abandoned at the golf course, and her fiancé kidnapped in a black piece of crap with four wheels, she shed more water beneath her eyelids.

If she failed to push forward with everything she had, she never stood a chance at success. Sure, she had failed at almost every corner and streetlight. Sure, failure pointed the barrel of its gun in her direction. But failure didn't stand a chance this time. She'd find a way to succeed, even if it meant she exhausted every last possibility. Even if she didn't have a damn clue how she'd do it.

CHAPTER 2

Ronnie Washington hated enclosed spaces. Ever since his older brother locked him in the closet for three hours when he was six years old, he developed a trauma-related condition, later identified as claustrophobia. For the next nineteen years of life, he picked up the scattered pieces of his phobia one at a time, until his body met the trunk of an Accord. Sure, it had more room than a Civic, but it wasn't meant for someone of his size. Crammed in the back with his knees jammed against his face, he scratched his nose with his black tuxedo pants and screamed against the fabric. Not that he wanted to, mind you. What he wanted to do was jump outside the trunk where the air was crisp, and he didn't feel ready to pass out from confusion and fear. Black spots and dark walls entered his brain, and he screamed again.

He kicked out with his shoes, and scuffed the black bastards—deposit included—in the process. He had bigger dreams and higher aspirations that dropped to the ground and rolled around, as he bumped the sides with every turn. Dreams disappeared into the black nothingness, and his nose did itch on multiple occasions. Just thinking about it made him want to scratch it, and then scratch it some more.

He hated his predicament. Not the least of which was the current trunk where he slipped in and out of consciousness every few minutes. His world revolved around rumbling, worn brake pads, and the noises of the road.

Ronnie didn't know how long he could survive in a trunk, because even his evil genius of a brother didn't resort to such extremes. One three-hour closet experience caused a lifetime of trauma and heated therapy sessions.

One dream after another slipped away from him, but at twenty-five years old, he planned to tame a few more demons before the fiends ate away at his insides. He shuddered at the thought of compassion and hadn't expected that particular gift to present itself, but it had—and when he last expected it. Elisha chewed tobacco and spewed four-letter words at the breakfast table, but her hair was blonde, and her eyes poked away at his insides.

How long had he been in the trunk? Fuck, he had no

idea. It didn't help that he blacked out for minutes at a time, and he experienced more bumps than a Kennywood coaster. He wore a watch, but the darn thing didn't glow-in-the-dark.

He had yelled at the beginning, but he realized rather quickly that the sound of the engine muffled his cries. So he kept those thoughts and opinions to himself, until the thoughts and opinions discovered a new voice and a new master. A mountain of thoughts overwhelmed him in the confined space—How long had he been in the trunk? How many times had he passed out? What time was it? Was he going to be okay? What happened to Elisha?—if he screamed like a girl, he couldn't help himself.

The vehicle clanked, and he bounced around. Either potholes filled the streets, or a shitty driver lingered behind the wheel. Sweat dripped into Ronnie's eyes, and his throat scratched whenever he opened his mouth. A sound exploded from the back of his throat before he could squelch it, and the thought of freedom died on his open lips. He even shed a few tears amidst the salt-stained sweat and plastered his shoulder against a series of tight turns.

He loved his fiancée more than he loved football and bumper cars. She had smiled—even with her tongue stuck—and looked at him with nothing but affection and warmth the first time he met her years ago on his way to trig class, and now that was gone too.

He hated these bastards, the two who had shown up in the midst of the ceremony and carted him away through the double doors. It depressed him. All of it. Instead of being excited, elated even, genuine fear ruled his eyes and heart, and it threatened to consume him from the inside out. Motivation filled his heart, and he kicked out again. The shoe, or his toe, broke, and he screamed out in pain. Screamed long enough against the wool fabric to finish off his voice while his mind turned blank and pain filled his heart and his head. He succumbed to it: his fate. Even if he failed in one miserable string of obscenities and madness entered his world, he'd charge forward beyond his current destination. Instead of a life filled with happiness and hope, something sinister entered the realm of his universe.

He'd find a way out of the blackness. Or he'd die trying.

The air charged around him. Suffocating him once more, and again he went under. The thought of death entered his mind and strangled him. He couldn't get rid of death's selfishness. Sure, he was bastard. Possibly even a genuine one. But he wanted to live, doggone it, and it sure as shit appeared he was headed in the opposite direction. He waved the white flag, and somehow it filled him up. He was in over his head. That much he knew. Probably didn't know it before, but then the world morphed around him and surprised the crap out of him. Blackness woke him up in the middle of the night.

The car veered and swerved and tossed him around. He jammed his knee against his lip and busted it open. Blood poured out of his mouth and all over his white shirt. The warm stickiness slipped down his chin and stuck to his pants and face. The walls closed in around him and smothered what was left of his spirit. An image formed in his mind—his first day of kindergarten where life was so young and innocent—the one that he had lost over time, and then managed to regain again. Before the men swarmed and pushed and shoved him, he was ready to take control of his life. Life handed him a live grenade and a tight space, and death loomed like the annual office cold. His life filled with hate and missed opportunity, and the one beautiful entity blew away like a kite in an ocean breeze.

Doggone amateurs. That was his last thought before he passed out again.

CHAPTER 3

Forty Minutes Earlier, Saturday 2:15 p.m.:

All of her friends attended the ceremony. And even some that weren't. Elisha picked the guest list carefully, revisited it on multiple occasions to ensure she covered all the cheerleaders and friends, and even vetted multiple names with her fiancé and family. The pom-poms, however, remained in the closet. She almost changed the location to an indoor setting until she came to her senses and nixed the fourth photographer and the second deejay.

She glided down the aisle with a five-foot train behind her and flowers nestled in her hair. The wind whispered through her blonde curls, and the smile on her face was genuine. She never felt happier than she did at this particular moment with a sea of friendly, familiar faces staring back at her.

Leading up to her wedding day, the stress reached a peak, before it discovered a new high. Her mother had the best of intentions, but she went about it with a hatchet and a chainsaw, and a screaming match or two ensued. Or maybe it was three. Her dad stepped in, and he'd nearly ended up with a busted chin, courtesy of a skillet wielded from an obscene angle. A bottle of scotch later, the mood lightened, and her mother tossed the skillet into the sink.

But none of that mattered now. The limousine arrived late, courtesy of a bridesmaid who had a little too much champagne while her hair was fixed and her nails were done. To stop her pounding heart, Elisha even had a drink as well. It calmed her nerves, and offered her cheeks a rosy glow. One drink led to a second one, but Elisha devoured lunch and even breakfast, and so her mind stopped running, and the Monongahela no longer held her scattered thoughts. Instead, she focused for the first time in her life, and she was more than ready to marry the luckiest man in the world. Her friends had said as much two nights ago at her bachelorette party while she wore a crown of penises on her head and drank hard liquor from dark glasses.

Her task list proved long and arduous, but she managed to check more than a few boxes with nearly a dozen cute guys, and the white wine turned red before shots of vodka followed and somewhere during the night a Mexican boilermaker entered the picture. The party ended with a Chippendale's show that had gotten a little out of control. A dressing room incident—and possible blowjob, that didn't necessarily involve her—ensued, and she'd ended up guilty by association. When her bridesmaid returned, her bra was missing in action. Those errant thoughts of a night to remember—or forget—ran through Elisha's mind as her legs shifted in time to the music, and the hardwood dance floor rose up to meet her.

Beauty and wonder surrounded her. A row of candles in little boxes on either side of the main aisle, flowers in front of her, and flowers behind, and a limousine on standby.

The crowd stood still and parted for her. All eyes turned in her direction, and little kids and even some adults pointed with outstretched fingers and mumbled kind words that the light breeze blew away. Her lips were tight, and so was her smile. She held her head high, and glided across a scatter of red petals.

The blond chairs and lit candles glistened in the early afternoon. Somehow, beauty endured despite the wind, and the several upturned chairs from earlier no longer entered the equation.

The walk, though, was the longest of her life. A number of adoring faces stared at her and made her life a swirl of emotions. The dichotomy nearly caused her mind to unravel, right before she spotted his face. Her fiancé.

All of it made sense then: the champagne and the Chippendale's dancers and the shots of Grey Goose. His smile caused an imperceptible stumble and tripped her up for just for an instant.

Her blue shoes stood tall beneath her white dress. The way her body glided down the aisle with all eyes focused in her direction seemed perfect, and the smile on her face felt both amazing and wondrous. She wanted to believe in something greater than the perfect wedding on the perfect day. Just for a moment. A flower brushed her scalp, and she offered the world another smile.

Each step felt lighter than the one before it. About halfway down the aisle, she walked on air, and her heart moved her feet for her. One particular thought of the perfect end to the perfect day answered her dreams, and the thought's pleasure filled her up as well. The pleasure proved instantaneous until it wasn't, and her heart filled with pride until it was ready to burst again. The pain in her side brought on by nerves no longer mattered, the dreams she had lost seemed trivial, and each hope proved more meaningful than the one before it. The faces in the crowd mattered.

She glowed and the love flowed, and each smile placed in her direction made her feel a little taller in her blue shoes. The compassion strengthened her resolve, and each thought took over from the one before it. The train of her thoughts moved, and so did she.

She had her arm linked with her dad's, and the world

parted, as she pushed through the thick air. Her lips moved, and then they didn't. A single dose of fear tripped over itself, and leaned a little too hard to the left before it passed.

She felt better than she had ever felt in her life. The dream of her outdoor ceremony in the light breeze would have died with her, if not for him. Light poured in her direction along with a few of her own tears. A series of happy ones that somehow made her feel both wonderful and terrible at the same time. As the tears flowed and her heart glowed, she remembered the first time she met Ronnie.

It was wonderful. Magical even. But not nearly as perfect as this day.

In high heels, she was just a bit shorter than her dad. She didn't know why that particular thought crossed her mind, or if it even mattered. Her hopes were high, and they ventured higher.

Her maid of honor smiled at her, and Elisha smiled back. The day couldn't have been more perfect if she'd picked it out herself. Other than the slight breeze, it was sixty degrees. The ceremony started, and her life changed. Her blue shoes moved, and so did she. Her mind raced, but she didn't attempt to chase after it. Her life felt complete and whole, and not necessarily all for show. Her life ahead was all that mattered.

Each opportunity took over at some point, and the

limousine ride disappeared into the recesses of her mind. The figment bobbed and dipped from existence, and one day this moment would pass like all the others.

She felt it, the instant the air changed. Her arm slipped from her dad's, and her whole world tilted on its axis. Her smile faded, before it disappeared altogether. The passion that led to compassion collapsed, and she was ready to give it all up for just a moment longer, until that particular moment was gone.

Elation and good cheer died at the altar.

CHAPTER 4

Saturday, 2:15 p.m.:

Ronnie flexed his shoulders, his best man at his side. He and his best man were inseparable for the better part of his life, ever since that first day of T-ball when the black helmet was bigger than his head, and his voice was so high he had to work to bring it back down. Ronnie should have been happy with his life, and he was. With the pastor behind him, and his best friend to his left, he thought of the soft grass and the white ball.

The mystical moment completed his existence and led him to think about heaven with the white pearly gates and the pickup truck. Thoughts of an afterlife helped him when he smacked his shoulders in the mirror as he got ready for the big day. His thoughts strayed at the most inopportune of times—like his wedding for instance—and drifted away from him when his passion flittered away. His belief system allowed him to hope and dream.

Standing in front of a crowd of familiar faces should have been the most wonderful moment of his life. But it wasn't.

The phone call he'd received moments before unsettled his already tenuous presence. The voice on the other end was a demon or fiend filled with harsh words and cruel promises, and the voice only grew stronger with time. The conversation ended in less than six minutes. It was the worst six minutes of his life, and now, instead of being happy and glad, he was left with emptiness inside. The midnight train headed out of town with him as the conductor, and he discovered the first crossroad of his life less than twenty minutes before his big moment.

The man was a comedian with the way he held everyone's attention. He had a big mouth and an even bigger personality. Persistence filled his face, and that persistence shoved forward with each passing instant. Significant promise filled each moment, until that promise bled onto the bathroom floor, the way he bled less than an hour before. A head wound. The bleeding surged out of control, the way all head wounds do, and now he hoped to put a few more pieces of the puzzle together. At least he stopped the bleeding without a giant patch on his forehead.

He needed drama free photos. The unconvincing nature of a brown patch above his right eye while his soon-to-be-wife sported a white wedding dress made his entire body cringe. Even the latest Photoshop software could have caused his entire plan to become undone. But the styptic pencil worked to perfection.

He bounced on the balls of his feet, as his beautiful bride walked down the aisle. The smile on his face was genuine. Everything else behind it was not. His life reminded him of the rose petals that danced across the white floor in the light breeze.

He had practiced his vows, just to ensure he uttered the words without a single hiccup. Public speaking—he couldn't stand it. He preferred being out of the spotlight, instead of standing right in the middle of it in a tuxedo and tie.

He should have seen the end appear louder than a billboard. But he structured his life around failure. One after another. Each mounted on the one before it. He kept his needs separated and his passion discarded on the floor beneath his feet. Instead of playing the hand he was dealt, he tried to trade in one hand for another. And he ended up a failure on multiple levels.

The tuxedo was rented, even his shoes were. The haircut was cheap. The undershirt wasn't secondhand, but it might as well have been. The socks had a hole in the toe, and even his smile exhibited falseness and a lack of pride. Whether or not he chose to pursue it, he'd have to punch out nearly as quickly as he punched in. The rice could wait, but Elisha couldn't. He held her eyes for an instant, and her face glowed with immediate recognition.

His phone buzzed in his pocket, but he didn't pick it up. Instead, his pocket shook, his mind raced, and his hand jolted against his side, as his thumb tapped away at his thigh. The tick in his left eye briefly subsided, but it was temporary, and he'd find himself right back in position once again. He glanced over his left shoulder and then held out his right hand as his fiancée drew near.

A spot above her head—a blur, really—caught his attention, and then a strange man jerked his arm away from hers. Elisha screamed, Ronnie screamed, and the strange man dragged him away. The guests screamed and plowed into one another, while a gun was fired at the sky. A deep voice commanded attention, while two strange men dragged him across the grass. Ronnie's feet bounced along behind him, the arms beneath his locked tight. His entire body went limp, and he managed to feel nothing. Or at least it felt like nothing.

More guns fired. Smoke and fog surrounded him, and the world dissolved into a blurry haze. The large man in front made him feel infinitely smaller. The leader proved both proud and pretentious at the same time. Ronnie had no idea who the hell he was.

He reached his hands up toward the sky. Or he tried to before he was locked between two bodies. He felt less and less sure of himself, and his legs jerked of their own volition. Ready to move forward, he was shoved back with a callused hand.

He recognized the end. Even as it came for him, he should have been smarter about it. He should have had a plan and an escape route on standby. The intentions of his captors were as clear to him as the hand from his bride that had slipped right through his fingers. His world matched the fate of that delicate hand.

His life could have worked out better. Instead, he'd end up with nothing.

CHAPTER 5

Saturday, 2:06 p.m.:

Elisha hated limos: the remote-controlled partitions and the gaudiness of a vehicle that never seemed to end. The way her spirit lifted and made her feel like she was better than she truly was. The back of this particular one held booze and miniature wineglasses and party streamers. She stuck her head through the roof with the help of three of her bridesmaids, and she sang and swayed and yelled, as her eyes roamed the stream of unfamiliar faces at a crowded intersection. Cheering ensued on the sidewalk, and a man with a touch of gray in his hair winked at her. The driver swerved to avoid an obvious obstacle, and she fell back into pairs of waiting hands. Still giddy with the newness of it all, she smiled at the soft hands that steadied her ass. Still happy enough to change the world, her hand fumbled around for the open bottle. Still crazy enough to think that she could, she touched a finger to her lips and kissed it.

A burning sensation attacked her stomach. Maybe it was fear or the possibility of hope. The driver asked her to get down, but his faraway voice was swept away in the melee.

The leather dug into her backside. Her butt chaffed against the leather and her thong underwear. Tossing all practicality out the window, she decided to really go for it, and that caused her current calamity. The seat caressed her butt, and her mind raced, and she couldn't drink enough champagne to extricate all of her problems. But she had to try. Dammit, she needed this. Her big day was upon her, and she needed to embrace it with everything she had. Whatever went wrong, she was prepared to face it. The thought of a potential glitch made the champagne seem even more enticing.

The limo arrived late. Either he was stuck in traffic, or the last of her bridesmaids with her hair astray, and her thoughts scattered in a million different directions, failed to remember the exact time of the wedding. Either way, Elisha savored the last of her freedom.

Hope led the charge with a battering ram. Fate was here, right beside her, and the beautiful sensation would help see her through. The liquor eased her mind and her spirit.

Her best friends gathered around her to the end. A beautiful feeling. With her white dress, her hair pulled back from her face and fastened above her head, the curls framed her cheekbones, and her smile as beautiful as it would ever be, she felt whole. Elisha gripped the hand of her maid of honor and gave it a light squeeze. This was the moment where it all came together. Being late or stuck in traffic, none of that mattered now. What mattered was her marriage and everything that would come after. Her life was about to find another gear.

Instead of being scared or frightened even, elation filled her heart. She'd heard about cold feet and runaway brides, but that wasn't the case here. Not this time. She longed to recite her vows and begin the rest of her life.

Elisha had prepared for this moment. Ever since she was eight years old, playing in the basement with four of her friends, three of which were here with her now, she filled her mind and a scrapbook with dresses and flowers and wedding marches.

A crazy tragedy managed to steal one of her best friends away, and she didn't come back. Maybe not ever. At least that's what her friend had said, and Elisha shouldn't have believed her. But she did. Elisha shouldn't have challenged her, but she did. The conflict haunted her, but she tried not to think about it, or focus on it, as the limousine veered right. She screamed out, and the bottle dropped from her right hand, spilled onto the floor and the seat opposite hers. She shook her head, but her hair stayed in place.

The cobwebs drifted out of her brain, and spattered on the seat beside her. The ride before her was filled with potholes and a Cadillac and two moments that bled together before the sensation was lost in the breeze. A gentle breeze brushed up against the limo before it poured through the open window. The limo turned once more, and she had no idea where they were. Or how drunk she was. But, hopefully, not so much, since her scheduled vows were less than ten minutes away.

An influenza scare canceled her honeymoon, and instead of ten days in the fun and sun, she was set to return to work three days later. Sure, that sucked ass, but the booze helped—the bottle of champagne that she finished on her own the night before, and the other one she started this morning before it was pulled away from her. She felt a smile creep across her face.

Elisha experienced butterflies in her blue shoes, as her bridesmaids pulled her toward the golf course. The man out front waved at her as she walked by.

Her feet exploded, as the front of her shoe ground against her big toe. She grimaced and waited for the pain to go away.

"Are you nervous?" her maid of honor asked.

Elisha's heels clattered on the gravel, as she shook her head.

A hair on the back of her neck stood at attention.

First, it was too hot, and then it was too cold. A minute later, she wasn't sure what to think. A car kicked up gravel as it skidded around her, and the woman behind the wheel smirked. The train behind her lifted up into the air.

She had danced for a living. Back before she had a change of heart and a change of career. Her new career proved much more stable than her old one. Despite her willingness to prance on stage in front of a live audience, the thought of standing in front of a crowd now made her sick to her stomach. The alcohol didn't help matters either.

Her stomach thundered, and her smile turned into a grimace.

CHAPTER 6

Eighteen Hours Earlier, Friday, 8:48 p.m.:

Ronnie hated losing even more than he loved winning. He lost for the sixth time in a row with a pair of jacks and a stack of chips. It tore him up inside: the losing. He had no idea how the hell he would win his money back. A hundred dollars migrated from his wallet to the table, and across the way to the man with the bald head and the mirrored sunglasses who sat opposite him. The man had about as much personality as a Corolla.

Green felt covered the table, and the back of his leather seat was warm. He pulled his hat down low on top of his head, as the bald man stared back at him. The woman with the tight bust handed him another mixed drink and left with her butt high in the air. The tray was steady, even if her hips weren't.

The glass windows opened to the rest of the casino, and he stared out at a sea of unfamiliar faces with a few familiar ones sprinkled around. A few of his friends played the slot machines or tried their luck at the black-jack tables with mixed results. The smoke from the poker room filtered out underneath the double glass doors, as the cigar man to his right blew a perfect cloud of smoke. Ronnie tried not to inhale.

"You lookin' to get lucky?" Cigar Man asked. A puff of smoke replaced the silence.

Ronnie checked his cards before he looked up. "What the hell are you talking about?"

"You really are a piece of shit," Cigar Man said. "That girl has a family. You know that, don't you?"

"Our cocktail waitress is a woman, and trust me, I don't know anything. Truly, I don't."

Cigar Man looked down at his cards and smirked before he tossed three chips on top of the pile. "Truly, you are a stupid piece of shit."

"Do I know you?" Ronnie asked.

Cigar Man nodded his head. "Yeah, I've seen you around before. Winning isn't really your strong suit."

"Yep, and you're a dick."

The dealer pushed two cards across the table and coughed into his left hand. Baldie took another look at his cards and nodded. He nodded his head so often it was no longer a tell. His cards could have been a straight flush or a complete bust. He hadn't opened his mouth either, except when he asked the waitress for two drinks in the span of twenty minutes. The last one arrived over fifteen minutes ago.

"Are we playing cards here or what?" Cigar Man asked.

Ronnie adjusted a button on the front of his shirt. "You even have to ask—"

"I almost feel bad taking your money."

"Why don't you keep your thoughts to yourself?" Ronnie said.

"If that's how you sleep at night—"

The chair jammed against his backside. "I don't actually. Getting married is a high stress environment. Thanks for asking."

"Don't lose your shit," Cigar Man said.

The dealer nodded his head in agreement. Baldie offered a curt nod as well.

"Is that a command?"

"Life is filled with simple solutions. You either get married, or you don't."

Ronnie rubbed his chin with his middle finger. "I'm sure."

"I had a thought—"

"What?"

"You don't want to hear it," Cigar Man said.

Ronnie glanced down at his cards before his eyes popped back up. His hand blew chunks. "You never had it to begin with."

Cigar Man lifted his chin, turned his head, and looked him in the eye. The stare was meant to disarm him, but Ronnie kept his shit together. Even with his thoughts scattered and his dreams shattered and his cards on life support, he wasn't about to give up just yet. The debit card in his wallet screamed for attention, and if he ran out of funds, the credit card would step into the fold. He'd take it to the next level if he had to, and he'd exceed even his highest expectations. Gambling wasn't gambling if he knew he would win. He'd turn around this losing streak, and he'd make the man with the stogie chew off the end of his own cigar.

He filled his life with expectations and promise, and he needed to plug in a few details. The cards often spoke for themselves, and not in a kind manner. But he could turn his luck right-side up.

Several of the cocktail waitresses knew his name, and the man at the door remembered his face. The dealer was new, along with all but the cigar man around him. Ronnie didn't remember the man's face, but he did recall the stench from the end of the tip. The man with the cigar crowded the cramped table. His belly was so big it rolled its way toward the green felt.

Ronnie closed his eyes, and lifted his chin. The fan blew a breeze on his forehead, and he turned his head away. Distance and time sided with his round chin, and neither worked particularly well. He picked his head up, shook out the dust, and punched the wooden table with a closed fist. The dealer shot him a harried glance. Cigar Man roared, and his belly shook.

Ronnie's relentless pursuit of monetary compensation saved him on more than one occasion, even if it was a road well-traveled and filled with ditches and the occasional brick wall. He dreamed of winning for some time now, even if that particular instant passed him by and ended up showing him the middle finger. The luck of the draw ended with a string of bad cards and bad conversation.

Cigar Man exhaled a cloud of smoke. "You need to get your shit together."

"I don't know what you're talking about," Ronnie said.

"You want to get married, don't you?"

Ronnie glanced down at his wrist. "You think you know me?"

"I know you're here, and she's somewhere else. If this is your idea of a bachelor party, you might want to reconsider."

Ronnie scanned the empty faces in the semi-crowded room. "What?"

"Your fellow compatriots haven't checked on you in over an hour—"

Ronnie tapped his wrist. "So?"

Cigar Man took an even larger puff. "You haven't moved in almost two—"

"What's your point?"

Cigar Man grinned so wide the stains on his teeth showed. "If you're looking for a loan, you've come to the right place."

Ronnie offered a suspicious look. "What makes you think I need a loan?"

"The wallet in your pocket's been stretched to its limits. You believe your luck is about to change, and I'm willing to take a risk."

The dealer stared off into the distance, and Baldie removed the buzzing phone from his pocket. Baldie checked the screen before he removed himself and his stack of chips from the premises.

"It could go either way. My luck."

Cigar Man nodded his head in a slow, deliberate manner. "True statement. What do you say we sweeten the pot?"

Ronnie's eyes lit up and then darkened. "You wouldn't."

"You gonna give up now with the rest of that cocktail still clutched in your hand? Can't say that I blame you. It is a rather duplicitous run of bad mojo. You might want to consider calling off the wedding altogether."

"You're crazy."

"Maybe I am," Cigar Man said. "But is that how you want to be remembered?"

Ronnie pushed his chair away from the table and stood up. "I'd prefer that I wasn't."

Cigar Man stuffed a hand in his pocket and pulled out a wad of hundreds over an inch thick. He fanned them out across the table. "Dreams do make things easier."

Ronnie contemplated his otherwise luckless existence up to this point. He knew his luck would change, just as surely as his friends would come for him, and his bride could light up an entire room with nothing but her smile. He sat back down.

Personal tragedy led him. That was the crux of it. Tragedy was a beautiful fool that sucked out his soul. He didn't know where better was located, and the fan of bills was more cash than he'd ever seen in his life. His whole life went to crap years ago when he was twenty-two—a terrible age to have his life turn sour—but there wasn't much he could do about it now. It was more like a gnawing pain in his backside.

He was about to get married, doggone it. Instead, it felt like his funeral march played in the background. He couldn't stop staring at the hundreds, or the man with the glowing red tip at the end of his mouth. Ronnie wanted the bills plain and simple.

He could have given his own eulogy. The end was that clear to him, but his butt stuck to the spot on the leather, and he reached his hand out for the smattering of bills. The dealer gave a slight shake of his head, but he tuned out the voice of reason and snatched the money before he changed his mind.

He had tuned out the Muzak at the start of the game, but now the saxophones and xylophones once more entered his head. The sounds were distinct and filled him with pleasure, and the bills in his hand warmed the inside of his palm. The waitress had offered a wink and a glance before she plopped his drink on the table and carted the empty glass away. Each sound took on a life of its own, and it was all so beautiful and wonderful—possibly amazing—before amazing blew its top, and left him on the side of the road with a flat tire.

When he entered the casino two hours ago, the rain came down like a funnel, and the umbrella he had stashed in his glove compartment was no longer there. Despite the money caressing his fingers, Ronnie felt the same empty-handed pangs now that had paved his entrance. The collar strangled his neck, and he sighed with foolish pride.

He felt defeated. "Do I have a choice?" he asked.

CHAPTER 7

Saturday, 2:52 p.m.:

Elisha chased after the car that swiped her fiancé. Her tires skidded on the hard surface. She lost control, as she veered toward the mountains and the guardrail. The speedometer read sixty-five, but her mind told her otherwise. Having the pickup all to herself, she focused on the white lines and winding road, her fiancé somewhere up ahead, and the music coming through the speakers that allowed her to hold it altogether. But she couldn't, and when she should have slowed down, she kept the pedal pressed to the floor. The spit cup beside her was nearly full. She pointed her nose forward, her hands gripped the wheel, and she kept her pickup in the highest gear around the latest bend.

The brakes whined, and her left foot kept time to the music. Life in the ghetto changed to a country station. The song blared through the radio, and the voice on the other end reached a shrill crescendo. The woman sang about good boys gone bad. Elisha glanced at the halo of flowers on the seat beside her and wiped another tear from her eye.

The gas tank was half-full when she started. It was even less so now. Her dress bunched up around her, and her thong underwear slid between her butt crack. The air around her resembled a refrigerator, but she didn't have the heart to turn it down. The yellow sun slid in through the windshield, and wrapped her in a warm embrace. Her toes felt as blue as her shoes.

She had a beautiful spirit. Or at least that's what she was told. Now she wasn't so sure. But all signs pointed forward, and all roads brought her closer to her goal. Her head exploded, her nose turned cold, and the plastic cup next to her filled to the brim. The stress of the chase emptied her mind, along with her gas tank. She had no idea what the future held, or if she was ready for it.

She remembered the way her fiancé's hand felt against her own.

The black car churned ahead on the half empty road, and her mouth burned. The singing cleared her throat, and the chewing tobacco lodged between her teeth and her cheek. The keys clacked in the ignition, and the wind whistled through the open window. Her tires bounced on top of the uneven pavement.

A dog in a convertible stuck his head out of the open window, and his whiskers blew in front of his face. The sticker on the bumper made reference to Obama.

The road ahead resembled an obstacle course filled with cars and potholes and second chances. The mountain on the left lifted its chin toward the heavens, and the drop-off to the right left her with a queasy, uneasy feeling. The singer on the radio crooned in short, staccato bursts. Elisha kept one foot on the gas and one on the brake, and she didn't know which one to push next. Her spirit had integrated with her open surroundings, and she was in tune with her new reality. Hope left her head, and despair filled the void.

Her cup congealed. Her cell phone buzzed on the seat beside her. Elisha ignored the call.

She was ill-prepared at first for the road trip, but desire alone compelled her forward. Her bladder felt like it was the size of a watermelon, but she shoved the urge aside. She shouldn't have held back—when the strange men appeared out of nowhere—but if it was all the same to her, she feared the worst and wanted nothing more than to catch the four-wheeled black piece of crap. Her mind surged, and the smallest details remained the largest part of the puzzle. Why was her fiancé taken? Who were the two strange men? Instead of leading her in one direction, her thoughts shoved her in another, and the pickup followed suit on the golden horizon.

She couldn't shut up during the limo ride and the long goodbye from the previous evening.

After the black car raced away with Ronnie in the trunk, her brother told her to chase after them as he tossed her the keys and the warm breeze turned cold. And now she had no one to talk to. A horn honked, and the dog with the whiskers barked. Her need for closure had gone unfulfilled. It was stronger than her hope led her to believe. She hated her life and her white dress and her idiot fiancé. If Ronnie hadn't been a damn idiot, she'd have already stated her vows underneath the gazebo in front of an Internet preacher who wore a beanie to block the sun. She wanted a cozy affair without all the hoopla, pomp, and circumstance. Instead of a cluster of cars in front and behind, a sea of green and dilapidated buildings on both sides of the road, and a ditch that was now several minutes behind her, she'd have dinner and dancing and a deejay to announce her to God and country.

During a break in the song, she lifted her cup to spit. The dog turned his head in her direction. Her wedding had blown up in her face—not the first time things took a new path—and commandeered a closed space high above the ground.

The leap of faith was stupendous and insurmountable in some cases, and in other cases it proved downright tragic. Moments of freedom lived and breathed together, and somehow supplemented each other. And she should have seen the madness coming. But she hadn't. Instead of running or hiding, she managed to survive with one foot on the gas and one eye on the speedometer. Her rearview mirror never seemed to catch her attention.

She focused on the way her dress felt against her skin. Her dress was handpicked and hand stitched, and leaned toward a tremendously wonderful experience, before it wasn't. She suffered with her mind laid bare, as the need for survival took control. It could have consumed her, this need, and she'd have been okay. Right when she least expected it.

Elisha tapped her horn around a hairpin turn.

CHAPTER 8

Saturday, 4:00 p.m.:

When the car moved, Ronnie moved. Shifting along in back, he groaned and waited, biding his time, and each thought that entered his brain turned around and left again with each shoulder smack or head bump. He shifted in a pattern, and he leaned into each warm embrace and kissed his kneecap on more than one occasion. To lift each thought he needed time, and the walls of injustice closed in around him. He screamed into his bent knee and shook his head with unbridled abandon. The floor rocked beneath him.

He pounded away at his bane existence. Another blackout was more than ready for him, but he held on to the grip of despair. His needs had gone unfulfilled, his mind was dazed and confused, and once in a while he even managed to stay in the present. He kept one thought right next to another, until the moment was gone, and he was left with nothing but distrust. If he abandoned all hope, he wouldn't know how to live with himself.

His right side ached more than his left.

He had loved, and he had lost, and now he was caught somewhere in the middle. In a valley where trage- dy and circumstance met, he had his beliefs—always bet on black, his fiancée was a better person than he was, and the bad eventually caught up to the good—that helped see him through. He was ready to believe in something great- er than himself, and his desperation climbed along with the engine whine. He was ready to take those chances even before the opportunity presented itself, and he was ready to hope and dream on some tragic stream of con- sciousness. He hated life more than he should and the darkness more than the dawn. One opportunity com- pounded on top of another, and he discovered the faintest bit of hope in his darkest moments.

Moments compounded one on top of another. Each one was extrapolated and analyzed for signs of life. The gray day folded in on itself, as the brakes slammed. The heavy air weighed him down, and the sounds of the road mocked him. He shut himself down, and defended against the inevitable. The trunk felt even smaller than he first remembered.

It was one hell of a ride, and the time that passed

couldn't have been more than an hour or two. The road wound down, as gravity shoved him toward the front. The ties around his arms and legs held firm, even as his circumstances shifted ever so slightly. The car jerked and throttled him, and the doggone driver did it on purpose. He filled his life up with thoughts and hopes and desires and lived each moment as if it were his last, even if a few more moments occurred while the road jostled and pummeled him from all angles. The voice of reason inside his head screamed out in protest.

A steady rain hammered the trunk.

He bent and broke and found himself moving and circling back. He rubbed the rope around his wrists against the side of the trunk but to no avail. Measured and beaten, he held back with a sort of resurgence as he moved forward one more time. He begged for a glimmer of hope, but he found no justice in the small space.

His concentration faded, and so did his dreams. His mind drifted to meticulous green pastures with white sand and streams of water and little white balls that flew over two hundred yards. He hated golfing. It was a bastard of a sport. Chasing a white ball made his head want to explode. It was stupid and complicated with a rule book thick enough to have revisions. The simple pleasures were not so simple at all. Challenges and repercussions and glances and past circumstances filled his mind, and his way of life shifted with each movement of the car.

The damn dogs discovered his scent and tracked his existence to an outdoor wedding where he stood just in front of the pastor. He knew he should have just let it go and walked away from the game of cards where the hands always managed to lean in the wrong direction. But he couldn't. Danger stood right in front of his eyes, and stared him down. He could have plundered, or he could have fallen. But falling wasn't the same as getting back up.

He should have hated it more: the bumpy ride of life. He had, in fact, hated it more.

CHAPTER 9

Saturday, 3:50 p.m.:

Elisha was realistic, pessimistic even. She pushed and pulled the pickup in whatever direction the road took her, and, whether or not she meant to, she filled her life with the faintest hint of hope.

The gap between the black car and hers remained constant even as the road and scenery around her changed.

The next song on the radio reminded her of him, and the words caused a tear to trickle down her cheek and her mouth to open involuntarily.

She felt empty and incomplete. Inconsolable. She hated her life, the pickup, her white wedding dress, the bow in her hair, and where the future planned to take her.

She once almost punched a bellhop over the matter of a dropped bag. She'd stopped her hand inches away from his face, walked out of the room, and slammed the door. He opened his mouth, but closed it before any words came out. Even in the sense of tragedy, she found herself both willing and able to meet the call. Motivation focused her attention time and again, as she marched toward the finish line.

She pushed herself forward. The pressure mounted in her head, as she climbed the mountain on one side and back down on the other. Her spirit lifted her up toward the heavens, as the pickup met the sky. Chasing down a dream larger than any she had ever faced before, she dealt with the tragic moment that had followed her from the golf course. Die and let die powered her through the mile markers.

The radio blared, and her teeth gritted. The past consumed her all over again. The sensation garnered steam and sliced through her like a razor blade. She whipped her head to the side around a particularly challenging turn. The gas pedal pushed itself to the floor, and her leg stiffened in the forward position. The pickup rocked. It shimmied and shook on a higher than normal center of gravity, and fields of grass rose around her. Her spirit shook, and a demon nearly broke her in half. Nothing was as it seemed, and all of her plans changed in an instant. Something was out of place. Amiss. Sensation roamed through her like a fog. Rain cascaded down on her windshield, and splattered in nickels and dimes. Big droplets. Little ones. It was all the same.

The road before her blurred in the gray and the rain. A car swerved out in front of her, as it misjudged the gap in traffic. She jerked the wheel, but not soon enough. She swerved. The car in front of her swerved, but in the same direction. The collision was profound and immediate. Crunching metal and bending glass. Shards scattered. Her dreams shattered. An explosion. The right side of her car imploded.

The impact crushed her passenger window. Her head bobbed, and the airbag exploded.

Dazed and shaken, she pulled herself from the wreckage. Cursing like a sailor, she opened her door and slid out through the gap. With her dream of freedom on the sideline, she marched in time, up and down the road on the right shoulder. Her arms flailed and wind milled, and the man beside her yelled in her ear. He uttered words that the wind and rain drifted away, and she stepped out of his close proximity. She clamped down, and shut herself off from the world. Her mind experienced a light haze.

She couldn't feel her hands, and both of her legs were numb. She stumbled and fell and tried to pick herself back up. She planted her palms on the ground, and her arms shook from either cold or adrenaline or both.

She fell again and rolled over in the grass until her eyes were pointed toward the sky.

Keeping her gaze heavenward, she said one silent prayer and then another. The man beside her bumped his foot against her. Rubbed against her in a suggestive manner with the toe of his shoe. He was big. Much bigger than she was and as wide as a desk. His hands were the size of clams. The smirk on his face was bigger than an oasis.

Several minutes later a siren sounded in the distance, and the world turned to a dark haze.

CHAPTER 10

Saturday, 6:15 p.m.:

The trunk popped open. Ronnie blinked. The light crushed his eyes and his spirit. He blinked again and turned his head away from the harsh reality. A hand smacked against his face. Once. Twice. He blinked once again and thrust his bound hands in front of him. He pushed his hands out but met only dead air and empty space. He was deadlifted out of his cubbyhole. He hung limply with his arms in front of him, still tied at the wrists. His eyes turned away. The world around him blurred.

The men before him were smaller than he remembered. Lanky. All arms and limbs and sticks with stern expressions and unfamiliar accents.

Ronnie was dazed, confused. Bruised and disoriented.

The arms around him released, and he flopped to the ground. He didn't roll around. He lay there, unmoving. Flat on his back, he closed his eyes one more time. He hoped the demons would disappear.

He opened his eyes and stared off into the distance. Not looking at anything in particular. He felt one sensation and then another. Each sensation rolled through him like a wave. His breathing was shallow. Non-existent. It resembled small hiccups over regular breaths.

It was evening. The dark smacked him in the face. A hand smacked him on the cheek. He could feel the pain all the way down in between his toes. They pulled him to his feet. But his legs buckled, and he dropped to the ground again. Four arms lifted him back up. He smacked hard into the chest of the man on his right, the smaller of the two small men. A mouth uttered words he didn't understand. He swayed.

He was distorted. Perplexed. He was downright incoherent for more than a moment. The need for survival materialized, and he was ready to face the dream and the demons all over again. To face the road ahead filled with potholes and roadblocks.

He placed his tied hands over his cheek and screamed. A hand reached out and grabbed him around the neck. He choked. Coughing and sputtering, he reached out his hands, and caught only dead air. He caught another current of air, and a stream of water attacked his face with precision. He was pushed and shoved around. The hands of time compressed before him and wrapped around his neck. His throat tightened.

The world around him blackened.

The dream of resistance filled his head. That was what he believed when the road before him changed, and each sensation piggybacked on the one before it. The thought of freedom developed. More than one belief had somehow taken hold as he moved and shook like a branch on a tree. The arms underneath him tightened, and his world constricted.

A metamorphosis occurred, and his thoughts turned to defeat. His spirit depleted, and he shook with anger and rage.

If he could just get past the slapping and backstabbing that had somehow taken over his world, the car rides and mass confusion that made him hate life. The tight spaces that caused his shoulder to ache and made him question his existence. Nothing was right: not his head or his heart. He slipped and slid across the plain, extending his hands toward the moon. A hand smacked it back down again. He bent over at the waist. The smack to the back of his head was vicious, and he stumbled forward. But his legs didn't buckle this time.

"You really are a bastard," a man said,

"I thought I didn't have a choice in the matter."

"You don't," the man replied.

"Are you trying to predict the future?" a second voice asked.

"Not hardly," Ronnie said.

He bent over at the waist again and heaved, and then he heaved again. His head rocked side to side, and then the blackness lingered. The hands of time took hold of him once more.

He wasn't sure about anything now. He thought he had it all figured out, but he didn't. He embraced the vast emptiness.

CHAPTER 11

Saturday, 5:54 p.m.:

Elisha was disoriented. Out of place. Her head spun in a million different directions. Both her room and hospital bed were white, and so were her clothes. The TV played a soap opera on low, one which she was unfamiliar with. A nurse checked on her on an infrequent basis, and the doctor assured her she would be fine. Her side pounded when she shifted atop the bed, and her head worked in tandem with her side.

The crash was spectacular. Epic even. It rocked her and blended the blackness of multiple hours into one. Her feelings were crushed on the pavement like a centipede, and she was more than a dollar short. Even if she wasn't quite ready, she was prepared to accept the challenge.

The doctor provided her with a series of memory exercises to aid in the recovery process.

Her mind flashed back to the pickup beaten beyond recognition, clinging to the side of the road in a heap of twisted metal and broken glass. It folded like an accordion on the passenger side, and the imprint of the car that struck her remained at the forefront of her cognizance. She was ready to give it all up in the name of love, to put the past behind her rather than have it take control of her universe. The man on the other side forgave her, and she might have been forgotten if it wasn't for the ragged road ahead. The car that struck her vanished shortly after the crash, and she was long gone from the temptation of the man with the foul mouth and harsh words who drifted in and out of her consciousness. Her knees had bent, her legs had buckled, and her vision had turned gray.

The other car was a squashed pumpkin. And she had ended up stuck to a stretcher with her arms wrapped around her chest and a blanket tucked underneath her chin. The hint of frost nipped in the breeze, smacked against her face, and mixed with the rain. The breeze. A strange man asked her name before he placed a mask around her face, and the world had faded to black.

Her room smelled of lemon and bleach, and she looked up at the ceiling and counted the tiles. She shouldn't live like this. In a strange room in a strange bed where a man in a blue uniform served her green Jell-O and cold meat on a plastic plate. Her memories shifted out of order, and her current medical condition led her mind astray. She didn't remember much either before or after the car crash, and the doctor informed her this was a normal occurrence.

A woman spoke in a monotone voice over the intercom.

Elisha couldn't have changed her life even if she wanted to. Predestined. Or at least it felt that way. She hated it. The freight train came toward her, and she had jerked out of the way. But not quick enough. She had ducked and covered as glass exploded around her, and plastic scrunched against metal. She had tensed up, even as the tension ultimately failed her. Even as she had ultimately failed herself. Her body felt like she had slammed into a brick wall at full speed, and her chest hurt more than the rest of her.

Her brain moved one step behind the rest of the world, even as she tried to get one step ahead. The gray came for her, and she raced to embrace it.

She spoke in hushed tones, as a man in a blue suit checked her out. Possibly a nice-looking man from what she remembered. He had a gentle face. A moment of uncertainty laid out in front of her, and she turned her frown upside down. That moment was now gone. Just like she was. She left the scene in the blink of flashing lights. The steady siren was all she heard.

Her backside turned stiff from reclining in the same

position, and the minutes ticked by on the clock on the wall next to the flat screen.

Even as the road divided, she found herself clinging to the intersection between this moment and the one after, and the gaps were what she hoped to understand.

But now nothing was certain. Now she juggled balls, dropped more than a few, and listened to the bed squeak when she moved. Voices and smells drifted through the open door, and the bed to her right was currently empty.

Her head had slammed against the side of the door, and she had brushed back blood from her eyes. Her skid marks covered the slick road.

The side window had buckled, and her mind had shattered. Sunshine and rainbows and pixie sticks gave her courage when she needed it the most. The man in the back of the ambulance called her miss and commented on her nice white dress. She hoped it hung in the closet.

Time to move on, that's what her mother had said. But then her mother was an idiot. She couldn't even keep her own life together, and her father followed the old cliché: He left her for a younger woman.

CHAPTER 12

Saturday, 8:37 p.m.:

The door to the room was locked. The room was dark, damp, and the blindfold pressed flush against his face. His cheeks were damp. There was an eerie silence, and the front of his chair rubbed against his back. The blackness seemed even more infinite. Time of day remained uncertain for him—maybe it had been an hour, or maybe it had been four—and the glorious moment of escape proved challenging, but he was ready for it.

Before they had blindfolded him and tied him to a chair, he had seen a mattress in one corner of the room, and a bucket in the other. The mattress was bare, but the bucket contained a foul smelling liquid at the bottom. It reminded him of expired milk. The aroma permeated throughout the room, and he gagged. Left to his own devices, he shrugged off the silence, and rubbed his hands up and down the back of the chair.

He only had a minute to gauge the entire room before a man slapped the blindfold in place, and his memories began to blend together. He licked his lips, and tasted salt on his tongue.

The door opened, and a single pair of footsteps crossed the threshold. The footsteps were heavy against the bare floor.

"You really are a sonofabitch," Ronnie said.

"And you're a stupid shit," the man said.

"You never said this would be such a challenge." Ronnie dipped his left shoulder. "Why am I here?"

A chair squeaked, and the strange man sat. "Would you have done it any differently?"

"I might have taken the high road," Ronnie said.

Shuffling cards filled the small space. The squeaking chair moved closer. Ronnie's back stiffened.

"Let's determine your fate," the man said.

Ronnie offered no reply.

A fan blew against his face, and he was punched in the gut. He bounced back and forward, and the bindings against his arms held. The second punch was worse than the first, and he doubled over. He spat, and sucked in a ragged breath. The monstrosity of the situation compounded before him.

He embraced his fate, whatever it entailed. His mind reeled, and he slipped into a confused dream where the dolphins gathered, or maybe it was whales. The waves dragged him farther away from shore, and the sun beat down against his head. A hard slap jarred him back to the present.

His cold and misty eyes searched out the eerie quiet that covered him like a blanket. The man blew warm air against his face, as the shuffled cards determined his fate.

He strained against the bindings one more time. The fan whirred overhead, and a stream of light entered below the blindfold. The man blew and the trees grew and his hands were intertwined against the back of the chair, and each sensation built on the one before it.

While the man was strange, the voice sounded familiar. A voice from his past, or an acquaintance from days long gone. The shuffling stopped. His head smacked against a hard object, and the chair pushed against him. The flick of the blade resounded loud inside his head. The strange man shoved the blindfold up, and a white light caused Ronnie to turn his head away. An arm lifted him to his feet. His legs gave way, and he was shoved across the room. The man shoved Ronnie's back against the wall. The blade whistled through the air, and struck just above his head.

A leather object, like a belt or a whip, pummeled him, and he screamed out loud. No one came to help. The man laughed at him, and the white light continued to blind him. Ronnie couldn't see the man's face. He sang to himself. He sang and hiccupped, and his mind hoped for an escape, and the sensation of pain filled his universe.

Nothing seemed to matter to the man as long as Ronnie was battered and stuffed like a goose into a brick oven. The man cackled in a high-pitched squeal as blood trickled down Ronnie's left arm. He welcomed death over pain. That was his last thought before he passed out.

When he came to, the lights in his head sparkled and crackled, and his synapses fired in a million different directions. The white light left the room, and the blindfold replaced it. The chair kept his arms firmly in place, and numbness covered his entire body.

The chair tipped over, and he smacked his head against wood or linoleum. A gash opened, blood trickled into his eyes, and a strange emptiness filled his insides.

He grew desperate. The screaming in his head reverberated louder. The voices were greater. He shook off a few cobwebs as a pinprick of light smashed his face. A figure loomed large on the other side. Labored breathing was all he heard.

The chair flipped again, and his legs touched solid ground. The figure bumped against the chair, and it rocked from side to side. The rocking stopped, and a fist smashed against the back of his head. It came with more force than a mallet, and his head jerked forward. Streams of light and dark danced in front of his face. He blinked and nearly lost consciousness once more. He grunted.

Nothing else mattered, but her. Elisha. She danced in a long, white dress inside his head. His bride. The one he was supposed to love until the end of time. The one he had left behind when two strange men dragged him away in front of his family, friends, and distant relatives.

The spots were brighter, and his eyes were wider, and the pinpricks danced in front of his face. The blindfold and bindings tightened, and the chasm between this moment and the next widened.

Screaming resounded inside his head, until he realized it was his own.

CHAPTER 13

Saturday, 8:22 p.m.:

Her universe was small, but Elisha wasn't in charge. In fact, she was catatonic for a moment, before her world came back into focus. Her arms flew up, and the IV in her arm popped free. A monitor beeped, she frowned, but the TV offered no reply.

A nurse in blue entered the room, and Elisha's moment of freedom vanished. A hard edge grounded her, and the back of the bed lifted to meet her. The nurse next to her bed smiled and shook her head.

One gift. The white lab coats were a nice touch, and the white walls matched the whites in her eyes, and horizontal lines crossed the width of the TV but only intermittently. Elisha's heart was stolen, and whether or not it climbed up out of the doldrums rested on her shoulders. Fate played one peculiar trick after another. Her stitches felt like pinpricks against her forehead. And the little man in the white lab coat came for her. He planned to take her away, or so he said. Despite his height, his voice was deep.

The bandages limited her motions, and the nurse placed the IV back firmly in place. It was one long ride with a never-ending vibe. The antiseptic smell in the room grew stronger. She wondered if this was a memory or reality.

She held her right hand with her left and visualized grabbing the sand, as time slipped away from her. She needed to act to save Ronnie, but she had a limited number of options. Her mind was open, and she couldn't fill in the details fast enough. Nothing but a steaming pile of manure filled the cobwebs of her head. The doctor had not yet released her.

An unfamiliar voice told her to face the challenge. She rolled to the side away from the nurse, and the voice on the TV occupied more than a few gaps.

Her left hand shifted in front of her face, and she glared at it. The lines blurred. She slipped in and out of consciousness. The nurse in the blue scrubs vanished, and darkness filled in the otherwise empty void.

One challenge after another chronicled her life, and she had accepted every single one that crossed her path, including the SUV with the wide jaw that had nearly swallowed her whole. The breaking glass entered her nightmares, and the pair of headlights posed a dominant threat. She tossed and turned, and her stomach churned beneath her. The food on the plastic plate had vanished some time ago.

Maybe she could find a way to get out of bed. She had drawn a line in the sand, and she had crossed it, right before she was shoved in the opposite direction. The figure above her bed loomed large, even if it was just a figment from her current nightmare.

She had caught one misstep after another, and her life slipped through her hands. That was the challenge. Even as night came and the TV changed, she was determined to right the next wrong in her life.

The resting went much better than she expected, and moments of time blurred together. When it came to the darkness and the wide night sky, she embraced the light that entered between the gaps in the blinds.

A building and streetlamp across the way added more light to the madness.

Her mouth closed tight, and she turned her head to the right. She coughed, sputtered, and reached for the cup of water on the plastic tray next to her bed. She sipped through the bent straw, before she set the cup back down. She reached her left arm up and placed her fingers around her neck. She massaged the sides. Her head jerked, and her hands moved, then she succumbed to a slumber of her own accord.

When she awoke once more, she stared at the ceiling. The tiles mingled together like cobwebs, and the cracks pushed at the back of her brain. She counted the tiles, until she was certain of the exact number. Her smile was forced. Incomplete.

Her head felt as if it had swelled to the size of a cantaloupe. And the bandage wrapped around half her face itched and pulled. One eye was closed, and she couldn't focus for long periods of time without drifting into a state of unconsciousness. One particular moment stood out in her mind. The moment of impact. It was just before sunset, and the road was broken and battered, just like she was. She had swerved to avoid a deer—or a merging vehicle, she wasn't sure—and a car had taken its place. The impact crushed her spirit, and water splattered toward her.

She paced the ground on unsteady legs, and a man yelled at her. Like the rain, his words dripped off her back. The black car escaped.

Not reaching her fiancé—that scared her the most.

CHAPTER 14

Ronnie was smacked, and smacked again. The strange man pummeled either side of his head with repeated regularity. Time mingled and mangled until it was one giant mesh, and spiders with long legs came for him. The nightmare resembled a familiar track, and periods of time covered his mind when he was left by himself. That was all he could think about: the spiders. Big ones. Little ones. Ones with giant teeth, and ones with not-so-giant fangs. He couldn't quite figure out how to fill in the blanks. The little details.

The bucket moved closer to him, and the blindfold lifted for brief periods. The black walls made the room appear smaller than it really was, and the foul stench made him gag on multiple occasions. The thought of Elisha provided him with a sense of purpose, and his conscious state faded from existence. He rubbed his hands up and down the back of the chair when his world didn't fade to black.

His eyes bled, or maybe that was his forehead? He tried to wipe the blood away with his hands, but the chair and the ties held him back. It mocked him, and a bitter feeling grew within his gut. The bitterness of defeat ate away at his insides, and the stench filled his nostrils with hate.

The all-consuming sensation overwhelmed him, and his world turned black. And then he was able to move. First, his hands, and then his feet, and then he stood up. He stepped forward, first one way across the room, and then the other. He opened his mouth. But no words came out. He gagged, and gagged again, but managed to keep from retching. Spittle flowed from his mouth. His eyes opened wider, light met his pupils, and his mind cleared. His spirit shifted beneath him, and so did the floor. The spiders. He couldn't get the image out of his mind. The floor clicked and clacked, and he covered his ears. Was he really free, or was this another part of the nightmare?

The cobwebs and the giant eyes and the long legs and the claustrophobia spilled through his mind, and he turned his head to the side. Saliva spilled from his mouth and struck the ground next to his feet.

He shivered. He hated spiders. Even the little ones.

And he was not himself. Not since he had been kidnapped. Not since he had ended up in the back of a trunk and was dragged off to God knows where by ghosts of the night. Dropped in a strange room in a strange place, he found himself one with his fears. Periods of emptiness followed periods of beatings, and every bone and muscle in his body ached. He retched and gagged in the open bucket, and the chair limited his movements. He couldn't have stood even if he wanted to.

He hated it. Life. Life was a motherfucker, and it hated him right back. It took everything, and now he was left with nothing. And he'd die right here. With the foul smell and the spiders and the strange man with the familiar voice. He just knew it.

He resigned himself to the beatings and the darkness and the strange man in the strange room.

It was special with Elisha, until it wasn't. But different wasn't a concept he was familiar with. Different made his head and his sides ache. He gagged and coughed, and his whole body shook.

"You're a bunch of bastards."

Nothing.

"Do you hear me?"

Nothing.

"What do you want?"

Still, nothing.

"Why don't you just kill me?"

He turned his head. He coughed, and blood came out of his mouth. It trickled onto his shirt. His eyes closed, and he slept. The darkness. It was a beautiful thought before it disappeared. A welcoming sensation filled the sanctimonious void, and the universe closed in around him. He welcomed the blindfold, and the black void.

The door opened, and a single pair of footsteps covered the silence.

Ronnie mumbled to himself. Numbness covered his entire body. Cold air rushed in. A chair squeaked and was dragged across the wood, and the strange man sat. He removed the blindfold, and Ronnie blinked. The man who sat across from him was tall and lanky, and he had a full head of hair. Black. And his face was dark or distorted. The black face resembled the black walls of the room. Anger grew inside of Ronnie like a cancer and bubbled toward the surface. His entire body shook from head to foot, and he strained against the ropes.

The strange man waited.

"What the hell do you want?" Ronnie asked.

The man leaned forward. "You."

"Why?"

The man was silent.

The silence extended, and Ronnie's mind distended. The spiders closed in, and he was more than ready to pass out all over again. Clicking and clacking filled the confines of his mind. Each breath he took was more labored than the one before it.

"You're a stupid sonofabitch," Ronnie said.

The silence lingered. The man shoved a hand in his pocket and produced a deck of cards.

Ronnie cried. He shed tears for the fourteenth time in his life. Not that he was counting. The spiders closed in tighter, and his thoughts jumbled together faster. He would die in this strange room in front of this unfamiliar man who gave out beatings like parking tickets. The sensations came one right after another. But the end never came. He never managed to fill in a few blanks. Silence wrapped its hands around his neck and squeezed.

Instead, he managed to fill his head with madness. Spiders and witches and wands. He would have grimaced if he had remembered how. But the only option that made any sense was to give up, and so the tears dripped down his face and chin.

The fan whirred overhead, and the chair beneath the man squeaked.

The man leaned forward once more and smacked Ronnie's forehead. The harsh blow left another mark, and he bumped against the back of the chair. The ring on the man's hand drew blood. A fresh wound opened, and Ronnie's right eye bled. He blinked at the numbing sensation, as the cold air from the fan blew in his direction. Ronnie shivered and bled, the chair squeaked, and the man stood up, and the door closed.

And then Ronnie cried for the fifteenth time in his life.

CHAPTER 15

S omehow the sonofabitch was still alive. That wasn't part of the plan. Ronnie Washington should have been dead by now. Wasted. Sucked into a time vortex where compassion and sensation were left on the side of the road. He was beaten, forgotten, and laid to waste on some chance run in the sun. He was picked up. At his own wedding, no less, while he waited for his bride with his arm outstretched and the smile on his face wide enough for the preacher to take notice. It was easy. Too easy. Griffin couldn't believe his good fortune.

A wrong righted, and the debt repaid. Gambling only provided a means to an end, not the end itself. The man with the cigar had paid Griffin with a stack of cash that was over an inch thick. The bills disappeared in the back pocket of his pants.

The cabin was in some forgotten part of West Virginia where there were more squirrels and deer than they were people. The road to get here hadn't been paved in over two decades, and frost still covered the ground. The air was thick, and there was a nip to it. The fan in the room had a mind of its own.

A snatch and grab. A stunned crowd. But what could they do? Griffin had a gun, and so did his partner. He had opened his jacket and played off the hushed sensations and loud gasps. He grinned, or at least he thought he had. And he waited for the bride to follow. To chase. To run. But she hadn't. Her mouth had opened, but no sound had come out. Like the crowd, his move stunned her, and her father gripped her elbow tighter before the handoff had taken place. And Griffin had smiled, because that was all he could think to do at the time. The grin showed his teeth.

It wasn't his first wedding. Or his first snatch and grab. But this one held special meaning. The stupid sonofabitch, Washington, thought he was immune to his debts. That was his first mistake, but it wasn't his last. He had mentioned to the man with the cigar he was getting married the next day, and he had offered up the exact time and location. The arrogant prick.

Washington had fallen into his waiting arms, and his

shoes dragged across the concrete. The stunned crowd didn't even flinch.

Griffin had believed, and he had achieved. Nothing would stop him. Nothing. He'd win, and he'd win again. A thousand deaths would take the place of one existence. He had dispersed fear in the crowd, and he had watched the world swallow itself whole. Chaos ensued behind his back, but he clicked the key fob, and the door to the black car opened for him.

He popped the trunk, shoved Washington inside, and slammed the lid. He closed the door, shifted the car in gear, and pressed the accelerator before his partner had even adjusted his position in the seat next to him.

He hated his partner. The shit. The man had a cleft chin and a gap between his teeth. The shit even had beady eyes. Little slits.

Griffin didn't even know Washington before today. That's the stupid game he played. A gun for hire paid with a thick stack of bills in the back of his pants. The man was an idiot. His partner. He couldn't even put a coherent sentence together through the gap in his teeth. He stuttered and stumbled, and Washington had bled from a cut to his forehead, courtesy of an errant elbow from Griffin's partner.

This particular adventure wasn't planned. It appeared out of nowhere, and he went with it. No one was coming for Washington. His damn fiancée might try, but she was an itty bitty thing, and she wasn't smart enough to put two and two together. Too pretty for her own good, and she wouldn't risk her fitted wedding dress. That's all Griffin knew. And that's all that mattered. Open and shut. Exposed—and then Washington drifted toward death. Griffin didn't know why, but why didn't matter. Answers only led to more questions, and he preferred the version of least resistance. He didn't really focus on what he needed the most. He had stopped with that shit a long time ago. The less he knew, the longer he survived. In the end, only survival mattered.

The stupid shit. Washington kept his mouth shut, and his eyes pointed up, when he was stuffed in the trunk. A vacant stare hid behind his eyes, right before Griffin slammed the lid shut.

His dreams weren't real. Neither were the monsters. He spit at the hooded figure in black, and offered up his middle finger as his only reply.

Griffin had to deal with monsters when he was little. When he was in grade school, he jerked himself awake in the dark. Night terrors. The screaming had continued for more than a minute until his mom or dad rushed in and calmed him down. When he was older, he attempted to hide the pain with cocaine. It made his whole body numb, until it didn't.

Even if he couldn't push past it, he'd somehow find a way around it. Perseverance. Despair filled the road ahead, and the one behind was filled with pain.

CHAPTER 16

Saturday, 10:36 p.m.:

The walls had closed in long ago. Elisha had found a way to stay alive and survive. Missed opportunities. Each one more confusing than the one before it. Her head rang and the bells clanged, and the wind blew, and there wasn't much else she knew. It was only a matter of time. The road was long, and she had barely survived as it were. Nothing might have been what she needed the most. But she wasn't sure what that was. The TV was turned in the opposite direction, and silence permeated throughout the whitewashed room. Determined not to lose focus, she stared straight ahead and tried to fill in all the gaps before the accident.

The world out the window was dark and dreary, and

the white walls were just as troublesome as where she had come from. Nothing was ever going to be the same again. That much she knew. The monitor beeped, and the IV dripped, and the needle in her arm itched.

Vague ideas filled her head, a sense of justice dominated her universe, and she swallowed whatever pride she had left. The nurse with the mustache returned, held her wrist, and looked down at his watch. Time wasn't on her side, but time continued to drift ahead. He left, but the empty sensation remained.

She took one last look at her surroundings, turned her head, lifted her body, and ran. The IV yanked free, the monitor projected a state of emergency, and the man in the hallway moved his head in her direction. She experienced triumph, until a solid object struck her.

The wall knocked her flat to the ground. Her arms flailed, and her nose bled, and her hands were turned at an odd angle, and so were her legs. She flailed about like a turtle on its back and wiped a glob of snot from underneath her nose. Her lip curled down, and her hip jerked out. She pinched her nostrils together to stop the bleeding.

After she lifted herself up, she uttered a series of four-letter words. Two nurses entered and held onto either side.

"Are you all right?" the first one asked.

"What the hell were you trying to do? Escape?"

She shook her head.

"Didn't take you for a runner," the second one said.

"You're safe. No one can harm you here."

Safety was far from her top priority. But she adjusted her agenda, and the world around her stood up and took notice.

The bathroom sink was clean, and so was her nose after she wiped it with a handful of paper towels. And her wrist wasn't broken. She checked, and so did a nurse. And the intercom turned on and a voice droned on for fifteen or twenty seconds. One nurse left, while the other helped her back to bed. The nurse slipped the IV back in place and checked on her while she lay in bed with her head turned toward the ceiling. A series of low moans followed by a few groans and then an elongated period of silence before the moans and groans started back up again. The moans and groans were from her, not the TV.

She tried to sleep but images of evil filled her mind, and the man in the cloak came for her with a stern expression and a complete lack of compassion. The straps to the bed tied her hands and feet, and she was shot in the arm with a long needle. The darkness finally came. The nurses changed. She closed her eyes and waited. But nothing happened. The intercom clicked, and another voice droned on and on.

Her head pounded hard, and the shot in the arm made her limp. Dreams escaped her. Her private room didn't feel at all private.

The night filled with foolish pride, and sounds toppled over each other. One on top of another, and thoughts of her fiancé and the crash meshed together, and she couldn't move her legs or arms, and the drugs came once more in the form of a cup filled with three pills. Each thought made her want to turn her head away, but she somehow asked them to stay. Leaving felt like her only option.

A gadget lifted her head, and she glanced up at a blank face with pockmarked skin. It was the face of a nurse she didn't recognize.

The wreck shouldn't have happened. The road wasn't slick, and she wasn't out of control.

CHAPTER 17

Sunday, 8:19 a.m.:

The sensation returned to Ronnie's arms and legs, the lights returned to his eyes, and he left the darkness behind. His head screamed, and the little voice laughed. He slept, and he drifted in and out of consciousness throughout the night.

He hadn't died. He wasn't really sure how. The room was still the same as it was before. He was still bound to the chair and left behind for long stretches of time. The light was intermittent at best—his only way to know what time it was—and the fan was consistent. The curtains were solid black. The blindfold shifted its position up and down his face. Spiders torpedoed up and down the walls. He was sure of it. On the other side of the door two men stood guard. The bolt on the door held his world in place. Two thugs managed to kidnap him in a moment of weakness and in front of a wedding full of witnesses.

His soul was lost. The leprechauns were more than just little men. One had come for him in the night. Ronnie had bared his teeth and bit his bottom lip. The little man had turned his head away and run off in the direction of the spiders.

The blackness suffocated him, and his throat constricted around the rather harsh sensation. Blood covered his chin and shirt, and his wrists were raw underneath the rope.

Where was his fiancée? She should have come for him by now. Someone should have come for him by now. Witnesses blanketed the wedding and the early afternoon. Plenty of scared, tortured souls had opened their mouths and run in conflicting directions. He wanted to live through another day where the chilled air blew across his face.

The food was bland, and an ache leapt from the back of his hand. The men of the night departed, and the door slammed shut. The walls talked to him in his sleep, and he woke up screaming more than once. He woke up with his eyes bugged out of his head. His spirit crushed by the locked door, and the two men on the other side, with slits for eyes and hands large enough to squeeze the life out of him without even a second glance, waited with eager anticipation for the next torture session.

He hadn't seen much of the second man.

He should have killed himself when he had the chance. The thought crossed his mind more than one time, and he considered his otherwise limited existence.

The men would come through the door at any moment with blunt objects and long knives. He had bitten the man on the hand, but that only led to additional slaps to the face and cascading moments of anger. The whip and the bucket soon followed. He stopped worrying about his chafed wrists, the slits in his eyes that burned into his brain, and the light that filtered through the cracks in the dark curtains. He didn't know how he had slept with his hands tied behind his back, but he had.

He wasn't ready for it. Not any of the darkness or confined spaces or possible realities. It was impossible. Escape. And he believed in the particular possibilities of life.

The man in the cloak appeared again. The demon, with the long hands, bony fingers, and the mask that covered more than half his face, parted his lips. The apparition vanished, and the man with the split chin stood before him. Ronnie wasn't sure which man he hated more.

"I loathe your very existence," Ronnie said.

"Them's fighting words my friend."

"I was never your friend."

"Maybe not," the man said. "Maybe so."

"Why?"

"You already asked that question bub," the man said. "What makes you think you're going to get a different answer this time? You feelin' lucky?"

"If I was lucky, I wouldn't be here."

"True. True. You feeling blue?"

Ronnie stared hard at the chin. "I hate you."

The man's teeth gleamed. "You have to know me to hate me."

"What makes you think I don't?"

The slap came, and with it the pain. It shuddered through Ronnie. Tore through him like a tornado, and compressed his chest. He had taken the slap, and not been beaten back. He was ready to deal with the pain. He welcomed the harsh sensation. He wanted to avoid the spiders.

The man was still there. And he still looked like he was three screws to the wind and working on a fourth. Curious. The damn air conditioner was busted, and the fan droned on through the night. It clicked at a steady pace.

Ronnie turned his eyes to the ground. Looking for spiders in the midst of despair. None. He scoured the floor just in case.

When he popped his head back up more than a minute later, the man was gone.

CHAPTER 18

Y ou breaking out of this joint?" the woman with the open-backed-gown asked. What she lacked in stature, she made up for with a booming voice. The grit leapt from her tongue and left her lips. With chopsticks in her hair and a mole on her chin, her face screamed for attention. The first hint of gray streaked through the black, and a white plaster cast clung to her left arm.

"What's it to you?" Elisha asked.

The woman raised her voice higher. "I want to go with you."

"I don't even know you."

The small woman took a large step forward. "But

you're about to get your freedom—"

"How do you—?"

"I heard you—"

"Your arm's broken," Elisha said.

The woman glanced down, as if for the first time. "So it is."

A stare down ensued, and Elisha kept her head and eyes level. She rose up in bed and lifted her head above the end of her foot. The table off to her right was empty, and the nurse had stuffed her clothes in the closet on three hangars instead of two. The wedding dress garnered its own hangar.

"I might be able to help you." The woman strode closer to the bed and stuck out her right hand. "I'm Laine."

"Elisha. You got a ride?"

"No," Laine said. Her eyes twinkled. "But I got money."

"What's that going to get us?"

"Our freedom," Laine insisted. "Unless you don't want it."

"Why do you think I'm breaking out?"

Laine inched closer and lowered her voice. "Because you're as crazy as I am."

Elisha grinned for the first time, since the vehicle with the red lights dropped her off at the emergency room doors. "Crazier."

She discovered the monitor woke up half the third

floor and caused a temporary setback in the nurse department. Security guards had barreled toward her and stood like soldiers on the other side of the divide. But Laine didn't seem to mind.

"It reminded me of Mardi Gras," Laine insisted. "But with guns."

Elisha peered up at the small woman. "Why me?"

"You're trying to survive," Laine said, "and you can't do it from the inside."

Elisha scrunched up half her face. "Do you even know the way out?"

Laine took another step closer, and the mood of the air changed. "I believe I do."

Elisha rubbed her forehead. "And you'd show it to me?"

Laine nodded, and her eyes grew big. "I been watching you."

"And what's that done for you?" Elisha asked.

Laine shrugged. "Not much. But I believe in second chances, and you're the only chance I got."

Elisha leaned forward. "Where's this money of yours?"

"I got it," Laine said. "I'm good for it."

Elisha rubbed her forehead one more time. "I want to see it."

When Laine whipped it out, Elisha nearly passed out. There were enough bills to start a forest fire. Twenties mainly. Maybe she could still track down her fiancé, assuming the beautiful bastard was still alive. A debatable point, considering the way he was dragged off with one arm underneath each of his, and the way her guests and family had all just stood there with open mouths and wide eyes. The way she had just stood there, frozen in place as the space between her and him widened. She would find this elusive road, and she would bring him home. Elisha had no idea how she had gotten here, other than the ambulance ride and flashing red lights, where here even was, when the white walls would end, and when the procession of nurses and doctors would let her go. Rather than wait it out and watch her happiness slip away, she had decided to discharge herself against medical advice with a stash of cash and the help of an unforeseen friend to aid her along her present course.

She didn't know what happened to her new-found friend. Laine disappeared after the money flash, after Elisha closed her eyes for less than thirty seconds. The room remained unchanged, even if the pain remained the same.

Her stomach was all twisted in knots, and her thoughts were all twisted together like a pretzel. The air hovered above her and suffocated her, and she swallowed back what was left of the emotional roller coaster.

The room with the rubber walls called, but she had walked by it in the middle of the night and nothing happened. And she thought about a call—or a plan to leave—but she couldn't remember a single number.

Elisha cursed at the ceiling. Monsters appeared in the cracks. She heard voices in her head. The nurses came. Elisha screamed. The drugs kicked through her system and pounded away at her brain. The lights went out in Charleston, her eyes rolled back in her head, and then it was all over. The space filled with emptiness and darkness.

Her friend was gone. And so was she. She signed herself out.

"I don't agree with this," the man in the white lab coat reiterated for the second time. "You could have a concussion and undiagnosed head trauma."

She held up the clipboard in her hand. "That's why I'm signing this."

The man in the white lab coat disappeared without another word. Once the man left, Laine reappeared in street clothes with a pair of keys dangling from her index finger.

Elisha grabbed her clothes on the three hangars, shimmied into some pants and a teal blouse Laine had found for her, grabbed her new friend, and made a beeline for the glass doors before she ended up right back in bed with a plastic plate and a bent straw to her right.

She clicked the strap in place behind the wheel of an unfamiliar automobile. She didn't know where Laine had gotten the car and didn't care. A haze covered the glass and her mind, and a rather loud voice urged her to start the car. The voice was filled with insistence and extreme confidence, and the fog continued to clear.

What mattered was that she had survived. What mattered was that her fiancé was out there somewhere, and she was behind a wheel with a half-baked plan to bust him out.

The car started on the first try. She shifted the car into gear and left about a quarter-inch of rubber behind. She peeled out of the parking lot, nearly rear-ending an Accent, Accord, pickup, and Mercedes in that order. The front bumper bounced up and down, and she scraped the curb on the way out. She cringed, but she didn't back down. She didn't ease off the gas when a Lexus pulled out in front of her. Instead, she swerved into the left lane, and punched the gas with everything she had. She ran two red lights in a four block radius, and she was about to run a third when the person beside her screamed.

"What the hell do you think you're doing?"

She turned to look at the familiar voice and woman beside her. Laine. That was her name.

The fog cleared even more.

"Driving," Elisha said.

Laine gripped the handle against the door. "This is a suicide mission."

"If it was suicide, why did you offer to come along?"

Laine expunged a breath. "I didn't think you'd try to kill yourself."

"You got a problem with death?"

"You're a pain in the ass," Laine said,

"I happen to have one, thank you very much."

Laine faced straight ahead. "There was never a doubt in my mind."

"That mind have a coherent thought in it?" Elisha asked.

Laine punched the power button on the dashboard. "You plan on driving like a maniac this whole trip?"

Elisha gripped the steering wheel more tightly and whipped the car around a corner at an obscene angle. "I'm just trying to survive."

Laine turned up the volume. "You're not doing a very good job of it."

Another bout of silence ensued, and it was longer than the first. Elisha pushed forward with everything she had, and she wasn't feeling good about the truth or her particular situation. Her life was filled with rage, each instance more troubling than the one before it. She had moved when she should have stayed, and she had protested when she should have kept her mouth shut. But she didn't miss the nurses or the doctors with the probing questions. The feeling came back in her arms and legs.

Laine's voice resembled nails on a chalkboard. One hand. Dragging and stopping, and then dragging some more. The nails an extra-long sensation that conjured pain and suffering. The moments fixated one on top of another, and each challenge was better than the one before it. Rungs on a ladder, and all she needed to do was climb her way to the top. The roulette wheel of life, and she spun the ball with her left hand, instead of her right. Her hands were tied, and the situation was fried, and the road ahead was filled with orange cones and cruiser barriers. The sounds came down like voices all around, and the ones through the speakers took charge.

She lost control on the slick road, and the woman beside her screamed again. And then Elisha screamed too.

CHAPTER 19

Ronnie escaped. His arms pumped at his waist, and he moved until the stitch at his side began. He doubled over, clutched his stomach, and was more than ready to pass out. He coughed and hiccupped and his labored breathing came in gasps one right after another. Blood roared to his head. He turned his head upright, and he sprinted again. His arms pumped like pistons, the soles of his feet slammed against the asphalt and gravel, and he nearly tripped, but he managed to stay upright. He grimaced—he didn't know why—and the sensation of euphoria was all he had left.

How had it happened? He had loosened the ropes with his own blood, and the beatings had bled together, as time and space coexisted in one particular place. The spiders that crawled through the walls propelled him to further his cause, and the darkness forced him to put his feet to the floor and propel himself out the nearest door. After the series of beatings, the two guards had a mental meltdown, and he busted through the rickety door when he heard a rather loud snore.

The paper-thin walls made the spiders resemble monsters, and his mind filled in more than a few details. Adrenaline and fear pushed him forward, and an underestimation by the idiot guards paved his road to success. His knees locked, and he fell flat on his face. The ground kicked up at him and chipped away at his skin. Asphalt attacked his cheeks and busted his lip.

Coming to a road, his feet struck pavement. He lunged, and the momentum propelled him toward a trash container. Both he and the container struck the asphalt. The next thing he knew his ass was up in the air. He clutched the green bin for all he was worth. One photo snapped and then another. A kid with a pack and a phone made some comment that Ronnie couldn't comprehend, and another photo took the place of the one before it. He ran again. His feet pounded away, and his dreams of escape stood at the center of his universe. Each dream was more sublime than the one before it. The euphoria took hold, and he couldn't let it go. Voices pounded his mind with more force than a sledgehammer, as metal chipped away at the bone.

He dodged through trees and twigs, and a squirrel near the side of the road stopped to take notice. A bird called above him, but Ronnie didn't lift his head in that particular direction.

Two men. The one on the right had a heavier step than the one on his left, and the one on the left was about a half-step behind the one on the right. Ronnie should have remembered names, because he'd never forget faces. One yelled while the other was silent while Ronnie weaved his way through the trees. His reflection bounced off of a cabin window, and an overhead light struck the side of his face, and the landscape around him changed. The voices in his head began to speak in a foreign tongue. The language was unimportant.

The voice in his head grew louder than it had ever been before. The insistence was punctuated with exclamation points, and he shook off the droplets of doubt.

The ground buckled, or maybe that was his knee again. His face met solid ground with the ground winning. Compassion was not on his side, and neither was a positive attitude, even if the bells in his head resounded in unison. The squirrel turned his head in Ronnie's direction.

Ronnie brushed off his slacks and shoved forward. His hands weren't in the way this time, and neither was his mind.

With whatever thought he had left, he shifted hard to

the right, and tumbled down a hill. He ended up on his back in the middle of a bush, he shook his head, and tried to rid his mind of the spiders. The gigantic ones with the massive fangs.

He picked himself up, smacked his head into a tree, and went down hard. And this time he wasn't sure he could get back up. The world faded to black, as the footsteps lingered close behind. Two sets.

He wasn't sure how long he was out, but when he woke up the position of the sun had changed, and so had his shadow. A pool of drool—most of it had dried—covered his shirt, and the ground cover masked his existence. His legs were splayed, and one of his shoes was no longer attached to his sock. His hair felt as stiff as a preacher's spine.

The bliss wasn't of sound mind, and neither was he. The voice in his head pounded, and his shirt smelled. Or maybe it was his pants. An unfamiliar odor permeated from the trash bin, and the wooden bench next to him was covered in gum.

The escape led him to this spot, even if it wasn't his final destination. He just now found his stride, and possibly his voice as well. He couldn't say the journey was worth it, and he couldn't say he had enjoyed the ride, but he had learned from the road behind. The left side of his face felt more tender than the right, and the world shifted in and out of focus, depending on which eye he closed.

Familiar shouts rang through the air. Ronnie picked

both his head and his body up from the twigs. A lone streetlamp flickered in the distance. A breeze blew, and dirt rained down around him.

Familiar silhouettes rounded the turn, and he dove toward the uneven ground. Voices called, and gunshots followed. Ronnie slammed into another trash bin and pushed off with his right hand. Another shot rang out, pinged off the bin, and embedded itself in the tree just behind him. He covered his face with his hands as he ran and tripped over a root. The ground reached out to him, and he turned his head to the side. Dodging and weaving, he veered like the familiar drunk at the bar on his way out of town. He was hopeful and hurt at the same time, the feelings in his head weren't his conscious thoughts, and the sensations in his brain distorted his uneven mind. Even as his situation took a turn for the worse, he filled his head with the thought of Elisha and felt a sensation of happiness. It trickled through his head and fired on all synapses, and he was giddy from the waist down.

The hours had blended together, and so had the spiders. Nothing was ever going to be the same again.

Nothing.

CHAPTER 20

Sunday, 9:34 a.m.:

Elisha had lost all sense of purpose. She'd failed at every single thing she tried to accomplish. Tossed her spirit in a black hole and watched it spin into oblivion. But one feeling stood out above the rest. The feeling of insignificance. The feeling that she was doomed for the rest of her days, and every day beyond. She had wrecked one vehicle, and she was well on her way to wrecking this one, spinning out of control. The rubber gripped hard against the road, and silence filled the front compartment. Red lights loomed ahead, and the front of the car shimmied more than the back. Laine had jammed her fingernails against the dash, and the radio blared an unfamiliar tune.

Elisha hated her life. Her own wedding was in shambles. She couldn't find one single dove. Instead, moths and cocoons filled her world, and the terrible tragedy was bound to continue. And nothing was ever going to be the same again. The complete lack of empathy led her now, and the silhouettes of the men who had dragged her fiancé before she could finish her walk down the aisle filled her life with purpose.

She turned her head and smiled, and probably for the first time in her life, it actually meant something other than sarcasm. Because right now nothing meant everything to her. Nothing was what held her together. That and her sidekick with the incessant, booming voice that filled the enclosed space and surrounding vicinity. Laine was even louder than the radio.

The words and the vehicle both rumbled forward.

"Do you even know how to drive?" Laine asked.

Elisha's eyes flipped away from the road. "Of course."

"Then why are you swerving?"

"I'm thinking," Elisha said. She had lost about twelve hours, maybe more. The hours crumpled together, and the piece of paper that was her life went up in flames. Happiness drifted away from her and attached itself to another bumper.

"Maybe you should stick to driving."

Elisha gritted her teeth. "Are you trying to upset me?"

"Will it eliminate the swerving?"

"Will you forget the swerving?" Elisha said. "You're worse than my mother."

"At least she's still alive," Laine said.

"I'm sorry."

"I'm not," Laine retorted. "She was a real bastard."

Elisha's mother wasn't far behind. Elisha had missed more than a dozen calls from her, and she made up her mind not to return a single one.

She strangled the steering wheel. The plastic was nearly coming apart in her bare hands. Her knuckles were white, and her arms were rigid, and the thought of seeing her fiancé again kept her brain focused.

She had skimmed one parked car and nudged another. The second was turned in the opposite direction. She had gotten turned around when she had taken one too many right turns, and she was about to face the consequences of her actions—or her fiancé's idiotic mistakes—and maybe her thoughts weren't so convoluted after all.

How the fuck was she supposed to find her fiancé? Maybe he was a bastard like all the other bastards in her life. Like her father, and his father before him. Maybe she should just let Ronnie go, and maybe happiness would embrace her. Maybe this was her chance to start over.

She had his cell phone in her pocketbook. He had dropped it when he'd been dragged away, and the damn thing hadn't rung once. Ronnie was probably dead anyway. She had no idea why she even bothered to chase him anymore. It was easier to forget about him and move on with her life. Forget the bane of her existence, and the smiles he had placed on her face, and the challenges they had faced together, and the master plan of the two of them together. That would have been easier.

She was sure of it.

She needed her chewing tobacco, but she had dropped it at the scene of her previous crime when her world collided in a compilation of screeching metal, burning rubber, and broken glass.

"I need to make a stop," Elisha said.

Laine's eyes went wide. "What?"

Elisha jerked the wheel hard to the right, and the car rocketed over the slight incline. The brick and mortar store was small in size, but it advertised all the basic necessities. She shoved the car in park and jerked open the door while the engine continued to run in place.

Laine whipped her head to the left. "Where do you think you're going?"

Elisha was already halfway across the parking lot and didn't hear her.

Seven minutes later, she returned with a can of chewing tobacco and a paper cup. She slid behind the wheel and dropped the can and the cup next to each other.

Laine hadn't moved. "What. Is. That?"

Elisha spit in the cup. "I have a condition—"

"Oral cancer."

Elisha put the car in gear and stepped on the gas. "Tobacco soothes me."

Laine gagged, and her entire body moved with her. "It also causes crooked teeth."

Elisha ignored her.

If the damn plan hadn't blown up, it might have ended by now. The voices in her head were louder than the voices outside of her brain, and there were images she had witnessed, spirits she had called upon, and drugs she had taken. Morphine was her favorite. She liked to push the button on the IV drip.

She was wet and wild once. Carefree. In her teens, she'd been crazier than she was right now. Intense. That's what her parents had called her. She had pushed her body to the limit with cross country, out in the woods and between the trees, over rocks and roots and unstable ground. She finished third more often than she could count, and it did help her confidence when she skirted across that invisible line with a pack of girls behind her.

She had smiled once. She was sure of it. The car shook. Shimmied. Danced across the yellow line, and with the time it took her to get back across, she could have discovered the cure for cancer.

A pair of headlights darted toward her, and she jerked the wheel just in time.

"What do you think you're doing?" Laine asked.

"Driving."

"Not very well," Laine remarked.

Elisha tapped the wheel with her fingers. "I never claimed to be an expert."

Laine gripped the handle on the passenger door. "You might want to at least pretend."

"Are you a critic now?" Elisha asked.

"I'm not anything."

The clicking of the air conditioner kept a different beat than the radio, and Elisha's spirit sank. The winding road drifted, and she shifted right along with it. The gas gauge informed her she still had plenty of miles left in the tank.

"I have to find him," Elisha said.

"You're not going to do it by wrecking into parked vehicles."

"Would you like to drive?" Elisha asked.

"I haven't had a license in six months."

Elisha didn't ask the obvious question. "How do you get around?" She paused. "Never mind. I don't want to know."

The road vibrated beneath her, and she bounced along in syncopated rhythm. Elisha turned a vent toward her face and waited for her pseudo partner to complain about the cold. It didn't happen.

Her thoughts drifted toward the past. Her first boy-friend. The first time she'd had sex. The first time she'd sprinted toward the finish. The first time she'd actually managed to win a race. The first time what she wanted had passed right on by, and she didn't have the courage to stop it.

She had driven with purpose. Desire. With a cell phone in her pocketbook, a stranger beside her, and a driver's license somewhere in her wallet, or the glove compartment, or maybe she had lost it altogether. But it didn't matter none, as long as she managed to finish what she had started.

The morphine and concussion explained the lapses in her memory, and the unkind nurse with the stiff upper lip who had jerked in the IV with a little extra force. The way the cop had smiled, the way he had tilted his head, the way he had picked her up, and lifted her onto the gurney. It was an image she wouldn't soon forget, even if a few of the details had turned rather hazy.

CHAPTER 21

Ronnie Washington was a sonofabitch. Possibly a dead one. There was only so far he could run with a stitch in his side and blood dripping down the back of his leg. The rat bastard managed to survive this long on sheer will and instinct. But Washington wouldn't survive another hour. Let alone two.

He should have died already with his throat slit and the blood pooled. But execution was never an arbitrary phenomenon. Griffin liked orders. Ever since the military when he made his bed with a hard crease and bounced pennies off his mattress just for fun, he survived through the sheer order of the system.

Griffin was bound and determined not to lose, to run

a little faster and jump a little higher than the next guy. Motivation. He'd starved most of his life. He'd lived paycheck to paycheck on purpose. The hunger. He never wanted to forget what that was like. His orders came in manila envelopes, and he never questioned the invisible hand on the opposite end of the spectrum.

He was green once. On the first job. He'd walked on glass and bounded through plaster covered walls with his hip and his fist. He was made of steel. Or malleable plastic that bent in about six different directions and never broke.

He'd never had what he would call a normal relationship. His wife had big eyes and a big smile, and she was just plain big. She also liked to sleep around with a few other fellas when the mood struck her, and it often did. He focused on her needs and whatnot, and he never really made time for himself. She was a taker. That one. Giving was a trivial concept, and he lost his lottery ticket in the back of the sofa cushion.

Ten thousand dollars was pocket change to Bill Gates, but in Griffin's world it turned on the lights and kept the car running. As for passion, he manufactured it in droves and common sense. The way his wife said she had manufactured the full extent of their relationship. She left him for dead behind the wheel of a burnt automobile.

That sonofabitch Washington was a runner. That much was certain. The little shit ran like he was shot in the ass with a pellet gun. That made Griffin happy. The ass shooting. He hadn't expected the little shit to run like he'd been shot out of a cannon with a trail of smoke fifty feet behind him.

Griffin manufactured hate when he needed to. And he hated the little shit with everything he had. The one with an Oklahoma sized mouth. Washington leaned in whatever direction he wanted with his bleeding carcass and smug expression. It was all a complete wreck, and Washington somehow led the charge. The runner was drugged enough to shortchange an elephant, but still Washington was on his feet, and moving, and shaking in the breeze as he favored his left side.

Griffin's partner was an idiot. Griffin didn't even know why he had to deal with the shit. But circumstance determined Griffin's true fate. He had a revolver, when he needed the extra firepower, and determination when the revolver failed him.

His feet slammed against the soil, and he nearly twisted his ankle on the uneven ground. His knee gave way, and he dropped to the dirt. His feet slammed against the debris and broken branches, but he shoved himself forward with his chin held high. His partner huffed and puffed beside him with a slow gait and a hard wheeze. The man breathed harder than a tenor sax, and then he belched, and then the spirits called to him in an alcohol induced stupor. He coughed and sputtered like a madman with the force of a heavy rain.

The silver chain slammed against Griffin's chest, and his watch slammed against his wrist. A string of curse words spewed forth from his lips. His feet bounced, and so did his lungs, and his mind raced, and the trees narrowed, and his thoughts constricted.

Griffin peered around a pine tree with his hand on the bark. Washington was face up in the middle of a creek, and he snored like he had a sinus infection. His partner nudged him as he passed by. Griffin jerked the idiot's shirt, and yanked him back about two feet.

Griffin should have had the damn girl by now. The fiancé was just one piece of the puzzle, and he was a dimwitted one at that. Washington had spirit—and not much else. The Cigar Man wanted to hold the girl for ransom. Get his money that way.

Gray covered his entire world. Griffin reached forward with his good hand and pulled the shit from the shallow creek.

CHAPTER 22

Sunday, 10:46 a.m.:

The day was long. Elisha was fearless, even when she should have been afraid. She was willing to see it through, even when it didn't matter anymore. First a pickup, and now a car, and the road ahead seemed rather far. The West Virginia turns reminded her of her life. First she headed in one direction before she ended up being pulled in another.

The car was a stick shift, and she downshifted with ease around the turns and bends through the mountains as the wind ricocheted around her. The voice in her head screamed louder, but the woman beside her remained silent. The way her thoughts scrambled and jumbled together, one thought seemed to trip over another. Find her fiancé and bring him back. That was all that mattered. Nothing else did. Her companion beside her had a mouth on her that could rival a radio announcer, but the temporary respite provided calmness. The radio filled in the silence.

She had a glob of chewing tobacco wedged in her jaw, and she had a cup beside her that was nearly one-quarter full, and a partner that was running on empty. Laine entered the world of the living once more. She had drifted off with her head turned toward the window, with a shirt jammed between her head and the glass, and her mouth opened wide. She snored like a banshee, but she was awake now, and the lingering silence filled Elisha with a sense of calm. The crushing blow of defeat filled her life with a snowy void that was both challenging and meaningful at the same time, and the sensation helped her find another piece of herself. She had lost her self-confidence somewhere along the way, and the current of life was bound to pick her back up. She had dusted herself off once, and wilted in place when she should have sprung forward. Her fiancé was a bastard, but he was her bastard, and she needed to find him, even if it meant she succumbed to a rather erratic fate.

With the boundaries of her life wound tight, she pressed her lips together and chewed on the glob of tobacco in her mouth. She frowned and stared straight ahead at the white lines.

While Laine was out, Elisha had formed a new plan

in her mind with the wide-open road and more than enough pavement to allow her mind to drift and wander. She remembered her fiancé had a night out with the boys before he prepared to say "I do." She had pulled to the side of the blacktop, and, in a moment of desperation, she had scrolled through the photos on Ronnie's phone. The one that stood out most for her was a man she had never seen before. He was bigger than the Monongahela River, and the corona in his mouth looked like it could have lasted nearly a decade.

Charles Town wasn't as close as she would have preferred, but she felt like this man might hold the missing stub between her and her fiancé. If he was still at the casino—a long shot she knew—she planned to find him, or if she couldn't, maybe someone there could help with the missing details.

I-68 dragged its way through West Virginia and Maryland on its way to DC, and it wound its way through more of the Appalachian Mountains than her and the little car she drove were ready to face. The elevation and the scenery changed, even if the road didn't change all that much. But she wasn't pointed in the direction she had been before, and it was only a matter of time before Laine figured it all out.

Laine turned in her seat, and opened her eyes wide. "Do you have any idea what you're doing?"

"Not exactly," Elisha said. "Do you?"

"I'm just following you. You're the one running this show."

"Are you sure that's a good idea?" Elisha asked.

Laine bit her bottom lip. "When this blows up, I can say I had a fun ride. I knew there was more to you than sterile walls and a remote-controlled bed."

Elisha sighed. "You don't know me."

"I'm not really sure I know you at all. But I knew I wanted to go with you."

Elisha adjusted the vent on her left to blow higher. "Good," she said.

Having already told Laine about her fiancé and the group of strange men who took him away, there was no need for a repeat performance. Instead, her companion's attention focused in another direction.

"Why are we looking here?" Laine asked. "This isn't where we were headed before I shut my eyes."

"It's as good a place to start as any." Elisha kept her eyes on the road. "I was wondering when you might bring it up."

Elisha told Laine about the casino in Charles Town where the horses raced and the slot machines glowed, and Ronnie had experienced one last hurrah with the boys. Laine snatched her fiancé's phone from the pocketbook in the back that had dropped to the floor. She dragged her finger across the screen, and the phone blazed to life. Elisha kept Laine in her peripheral vision, and hoped the woman wouldn't find anything even more incriminating on the device than that one particular photo.

Laine pushed her hand flat against the dashboard. "I'm not sure that's a good plan."

Elisha stared straight ahead. "It's the only plan we have."

"True," Laine said. "But will it work?"

"Maybe not. Maybe so. But I do know what will happen if I do nothing." Elisha sucked in her breath and held back the tears. "I try not to fail."

"You don't do a very good job of that either," Laine said. "You were already in one accident. I don't think you should head toward another. Emotional driving is not safe driving."

"You have to pay to play." Ronnie had told her that once when she was too scared to even sit at the table next to him, while the dealer dealt the cards.

"Is that on a bumper sticker?" Laine asked.

"I read it somewhere," Elisha lied.

Laine shook her head and grinned. "You really are a piece of shit."

"Is that why you're here?"

"Honestly," Laine said, "I have no idea. How I ended up in your room in the first place is still a mystery to me. The nurse must have mixed up my medications. It happens, you know."

"Then what good are you?"

"Again, I have no idea." Laine kept her hand flat

against the dashboard. "But right now, I'm all you've got."

Over two hours of interstate passed, as I-68 turned into I-70, and Elisha made her way down I-81 just before Hagerstown and on into Charles Town. Once she crossed the border from Maryland into West Virginia, the sleepy towns reminded her of home. The casino was off of a two-lane road where traffic was light and so were the stoplights. Strip malls were placed here and there along the way, and there was more open space than there were modern buildings.

She parked the car in the tower next to the casino where the parking was free. More spots were filled than she had expected, and the walk to the elevator was longer than she would have preferred.

"What's our plan?" Laine asked.

"I don't know," Elisha said. "But I'm sure I'll figure it out in the elevator."

"We're only going down two floors."

"That's more than enough time," Elisha said.

She arrived with Laine just outside the casino room floor and passed her ID to the guard behind the podium who had to squint down to check her credentials. Once he completed the task for each of them, Elisha started with her prepared remarks.

"Do you know this man?" Elisha asked.

"Is that your phone?" the guard asked.

"No, it is not. It's my fiancé's."

"He was kidnapped," Laine added.

The guard's eyes widened. He peered down at the phone even harder. "He comes in here every day. He's hard to miss. I haven't seen him yet."

"If you do, you'll know where to find us," Laine said. "We'll be winning at the slots. Just look for all the cheering."

Elisha shook her head. "You're rather optimistic."

"I'm here to win," Laine said, "otherwise, what the hell is the point?"

Laine didn't win, but she was real good at pretending. She plopped herself down at an empty stool, slid her card in the slot, and started pushing the buttons. Elisha, on the other hand, scanned the room like she was a farmer and the herd were the cattle, looking for the ones with the biggest tales to tell.

Like the first interview, she struck out with the next two. On the fourth, she hit pay dirt. "I do know that man," the woman said. She said her name was Jill. She was in her twenties, and she had on an outfit that looked like it was made just for her. "He's a sonofabitch."

Elisha waited for the elaboration. She didn't have to wait long.

"I lost over a thousand dollars to him, and it wouldn't surprise me if the same thing happened to your fiancé. He's a liar, cheater, and a pervert. I can't believe he's not banned from here. He also bragged to me about how big his cabin was and where it was located. He's taken a few of his victims there, when they couldn't pay, or so he told me."

"Did you tell the police any of this?" Elisha asked.

Jill nodded. "Absolutely. But the cops said I couldn't press charges because I didn't have any physical evidence, and it was just my word against his. Plus, the man has more money than the devil himself, and he might even have the grin as well. If your fiancé is still alive, you'll probably find him there."

It wasn't much, but it was more than she had three hours ago. Elisha thanked Jill.

"Happy to help," Jill said. "I hope you catch the asshole."

CHAPTER 23

Sunday, 2:13 p.m.:

She was coming for him. Ronnie hadn't had much to look forward to, and he had no idea how he knew. But she was close. He could feel it. Feeling her way around in the dark, stumbling through the morning and afternoon fueled by sheer will and determination and the lingering sensation of hope. Elisha was nothing if not determined.

Dragged away from the creek and pulled once more toward the cabin at the end of a paved road on the outskirts of a small West Virginia town, he was hogtied and bound in the back of a moving vehicle for the second time in his life. Darkness cloaked over his world, and the two men in the front hadn't said much. The car had rumbled and shifted, as it wound around the mountains, and the paved road had turned to stone. The gaps between cars were real, and his mind filled with nightmare scenarios. The spiders were back, and so was the leprechaun. He couldn't decide which one was worse.

The cabin had been abandoned by the two men when Ronnie had taken off at a dead run, and the heat turned off on its own. The key to the front slid into the lock, and Ronnie heard the click that would seal his fate. A third man must have provided a script, and these men were merely actors in a predetermined play. Ronnie thought of the man with the stogie from the night before, and the multitude of bills that had been fanned out across the green felt. The strange man had spotted a weakness and gone for it. It had worked. The voice in Ronnie's head rained down from above, and his hands shook behind his back. He hated the strange man and his master plan. It was only money. It wasn't like Ronnie wouldn't pay him back. He just needed more time. The man had scared the piss out of him, and then Ronnie's worst nightmare had become reality.

The ropes were tighter than before, and he shifted in the chair. He had been dragged from the car into the cabin against his own volition, but after the slapping around and the running, he didn't have much fight left in him. He just hoped the man with the cigar would determine his fate sooner rather than later.

The two men found coffee grounds and canned

beans—Ronnie smelled the coffee followed by the beans—and the wooden rocker off to his right rocked back and forth of its own accord. The wood in the fireplace burned to embers, and the voices in the kitchen argued back and forth. He stared hard at the door and willed it to open, but the door didn't speak in return.

He had his eyes closed for as long as possible and dreamed of cornfields and rain that might help wash away all the pain. The stench of dry rot sifted through his nostrils and danced around in his sinus cavity. He wasn't particularly proud of his thoughts—dying right now sounded a whole lot better than living—and gestures. He wanted to give the world the middle finger. And he wasn't sure what would happen next. He didn't even know if he had a dog in the fight, or if there was any fight left in the dog, or the speed of the automobile as it had careened along the highway and bounced off the guardrail on its way toward the cabin. Plastic had rubbed against metal, and his eardrums vibrated in response. He had cringed, and the men in the front had cackled.

The boundaries of his life slipped through his fingers. All of it was out of his control. His fate was in the hands of two strange men in the cabin in a remote part of West Virginia. He wasn't particularly happy with his odds.

Control. It prevented him from finding the truth. Paper rustled, his head turned, and the chair scraped. The voices in the kitchen lingered in the small space, little feet skittered on the wooden porch, and birds chirped. His mind raced right out of the gate, and his body tried to keep up, even though he was tied to an inanimate object.

He shrugged his shoulders, and ran his hands up and down against the back of the chair. His tired arms worked as fast as they could. He blinked, but his surroundings didn't change.

None of this should have happened. Especially this particular predicament. He had a need and direction in his life, and what led him astray was a winning streak gone amiss. The cards in his hand changed, and his mind couldn't keep up. Cigar Man had all of his money, along with the stack of chips Ronnie handed back to him after the hands went south even more.

The fish bit and so did he. He moved, but then so did the men. His feet churned against the wood, his lungs burned, and his heart pounded against his chest cavity. His mind raced, and so did his hands. He pressed forward, the chair tumbled, and his hands slammed against the wood. Wetness dripped down, and he ground his teeth in his mouth. His wrist was probably broken, after it had slammed against the wood and then the chair.

Even if it was the last thing he ever did, he vowed to fight until his expiration date.

The rat bastards. He had delivered on his various promises, and the encouragement remained virtually non-existent. Voices called out to him, but he ignored the words. He suffered through the blackness, and dragged his feet and the chair toward the closed door.

"Hey," a voice said. "What the hell do you think you're doing?"

Ronnie pushed himself onward.

Inches away from the front door, the first blow struck the back of his head. His head smashed the wood and his nose, probably broken for the first time in his life, and his breath whistled in response. The man shoved his head down even more and came around toward the front. A fist snapped out and struck Ronnie's left cheek. On the second strike, he turned his head to the right, and the fist whispered past his right ear. But the third came hard and fast, and he was unable to dodge the blow, especially since his lips were still inches away from the hardwood. He was yanked to his feet, chair and all, his head struck the back, and the room lit up in a flash of white light.

A hiss in the wind. Another nail in the coffin. And pain ensued. He ground his teeth, and his eyes closed.

The smart money bet on the other party. Had he been smart, he would've folded his hand.

A shot in the dark echoed through the afternoon, the stars would come, and the battle was won when the lights went out over West Virginia. He had analyzed the numbers, front and back, and bet on the wrong horse more than once.

He didn't have control over the situation. Instead,

control ripped him to shreds, and darkness took over his lonely world.

CHAPTER 24

Elisha slammed on the brakes. Gravel kicked up all around the vehicle, and her tires dug hard against the rocks. Two trees were off to the right with one off to the left. She sliced between them and whipped the car around to the left. More gravel kicked up, and Laine bounced against the passenger door.

"The cabin," Elisha said, "is right there. We found it. You see the black car over on the right-hand side." She pointed, and Laine nodded. "That's the one I've been chasing."

"But we need a plan—"

"Storm the wooden door. If I kick in the front door hard enough, I don't even need to knock."

Laine sighed. "That's idiotic."

"I never claimed to be intelligent." Elisha smirked. "Just persistent."

Laine sighed even louder. "But you did claim to know what you're doing."

Elisha nodded.

The cabin was right where Jill told her it would be, and the black car loomed like an evil monstrosity that had consumed her every thought and desire. The cabin was all one level, there was no front porch to speak of, and the roof was rotted in spots. The windows had a film over them, and the front door didn't look all that sturdy. The idea to kick in the door sounded better and better, the more she thought about it. She wouldn't let Laine talk her out of it.

Elisha charged the front door. It splintered, and she dove inside. She turned to her right, and came up swinging. The front room was empty, and so was the one after that. The silence punched at her, and her forehead pounded. Her hands danced at her sides, and in front of her face, and not a single sound was heard in the place.

Laine stood by her side stride for stride, even though Elisha had told her to wait in the car. Laine's mouth moved, but the words disappeared in the air. Elisha shook her head, shaking out the cobwebs and the pockets of rust. Her ears pounded, and so did her heart. A staccato rhythm. She pressed her lips together. Concentration smashed against her, and pounded away at her. Her ears rung, and time enveloped her. Her heart struck her chest loud enough that it was the only sound she heard. Her lips shivered. She slammed into a wall, as darkness continued to surround her.

In the kitchen an empty glass stood on top of the table. She grabbed a can of green beans from the cupboard and one of creamed corn. She didn't see any knives in the immediate vicinity, and even if she had, she didn't trust herself to use one. A rattling shivered through the walls, and the hairs on her arms stood up.

"What the hell are you doing?" Laine asked.

Elisha held a finger to her lips and shook her head. She handed one of the cans to Laine.

Elisha waited, but nothing changed, so she pushed ahead, and her feet dragged across the floor. Time moved ahead, and so did she. The order didn't matter. The black hole was a constant presence, and the satisfaction was short-lived. The moment was lost, and then it was recaptured.

The cabin felt familiar to her, even though she had never seen it before. Time was not on her side. It had descended upon her like a nightmare and swallowed her whole. Transported back in time to before the wedding and before she met Ronnie, she considered walking away now, even after she had come this far. But she felt a presence in the next room, and she wanted to finish what she started, so she continued onward.

Life.

The steady beat.

The constant pressure.

Animal heads stared at her, and the fan overhead whirred. She held her breath, and swallowed her pride. A motion out of the corner of her eye turned her head to the side. It was nothing more than an animal outside the window. But it helped focus her head.

She hated her life, but she had the opportunity to change.

The knob on the bedroom door rattled, and she shoved the door open. On the other side, a man she didn't know stood next to her fiancé with a hand around his neck and a gun pointed at his head. Laine gripped Elisha's shoulder tighter, and her world collapsed in on itself.

"Get away from him, you bastard," Elisha said.

The strange man squeezed tighter. The gun held steady. "What the hell do you think you're doing?"

Elisha charged the strange man and dropped her shoulder. Filled with adrenaline and persistence and fueled by rage, Elisha slammed into the strange man. A loud boom erupted in the confined space. She tumbled with him to the ground, shoved her body close enough to the man that he couldn't gain position, and slammed the can of beans against his nose. Blood spurted the front of his shirt. She smacked him again. With her elbow, she knocked the gun away. She jumped to her feet, and stood over him with her foot at the center of his chest.

"That's my fiancé," she said.

"I'm supposed to care—"

Laine fumbled with the knot before she untied Ronnie. She removed the blindfold next.

"You're a sonofabitch—"

With Elisha's attention focused elsewhere, the strange man picked up her leg and tossed her to the side. She struck the hardwood and uttered a whispered breath. Another man entered the room, as large as the first. The first man dove for the gun. Elisha lunged. She was able to gain position once more along with the gun. The can of beans dropped to the floor. She kicked it toward the other side of the room.

"The fuck?" the second man said.

Before the man said another word, Laine knocked him out cold with the can of corn. The can struck the side of his head and then the ground with a thud. Elisha smiled.

"He owes Cigar Man ten grand," the strange man said. Blood oozed from his lips and down the front of his shirt.

"You're gonna beat it out of him?" Elisha asked.

"Cigar Man figured you'd find us."

Elisha grimaced. "He didn't know jack shit."

"You're a feisty one," the strange man said.

The two men were bonafide bastards. Ronnie might

have had debts to repay, but there were better ways to remedy the situation. A black hole formed at the pit of her stomach, and her mind strayed. The surprise grab had turned her mind blank, and emptiness filled the small space. But now the cobwebs disappeared, her mind cleared, and only sadness remained.

"You didn't think you'd win, did you?"

"You've got spunk," the first man said, "I'll give you that much." He took a step closer.

The pieces clicked into place like those of a jigsaw puzzle. The grip dug into her palm, and the air wrapped its hands around her neck. "You're an even bigger asshole. You were at the goddamn wedding."

"I was supposed to be."

"You weren't fucking invited," Elisha said. "I made up the guest list myself, and you weren't on it."

The strange man rubbed his jaw. "Maybe that's why I was left off. If Ronnie had paid his debts like a good little boy, none of this would have happened."

"The cabin in the woods was a nice touch. But I'm smarter than you are."

The strange man's eyes drifted down before he looked at her once more and took another step closer. "You tryin' to push my buttons?"

She placed her other hand on the grip. "Don't move," she said.

The man shrugged.

"Your kidnapping skills are severely lacking. Looks

like his wrist was broken along with his nose."

"A debt is a debt. That's all I have to say. You're still playing from a different deck of cards."

She gritted her teeth. "You're a fucking idiot."

The man smiled wide. "Your boyfriend?"

"You mean fiancé—"

"Whatever."

Elisha still couldn't believe any of this. Her brain still needed to catch up with the rest of her. "Your friend?" she asked.

The second one still hadn't moved from his face-down position after the blow to the side of his head.

The first man shrugged. "He's disposable."

"Like my fiancé?"

"For ten grand?" the man said. "Absolutely."

Elisha could smell his breath, even though she stood a few feet away from him. "You're fucking loaded."

"I've had a few. So what?"

"You're a bigger shithead than I ever—"

He charged. Elisha pulled the trigger. The sound was like being next to the coffee grinder in Starbucks. It pounded her ears, and the tears flowed. Streaming down her cheek, the droplets struck the floor one after another. The riverbed reached the hardwood and puddled there. Each tear was bigger than the one before it.

Ronnie touched her shoulder with his good hand, and she leaned toward him.

Laine placed a hand on her other shoulder. "Are you okay?"

"Who's your friend?" Ronnie asked.

"Someone I picked up along the way. Ronnie, this is Laine. I couldn't have made it this far without her."

"You're crazy, you know," Ronnie said. "Where's your dress?"

"It's in the car," Elisha said. "It'll need to be dry-cleaned."

"You're an idiot," Laine said. "You could've gotten yourself killed."

Elisha placed her hand on top of Laine's. "I'm still here, aren't I?"

Laine glared, and the air in the room changed. "So you say."

"I'm going to stick around this time," Ronnie said. "I'll also stop visiting the casinos. Believe I've learned my lesson, doggone it."

Elisha peered up at him. "You sure about that?"

Ronnie nodded. "Absolutely."

Laine sneezed. "If you kiss her, I'm out of here."

"Bless you," Ronnie said.

"You're looking for something that isn't there." Elisha searched Ronnie's eyes. "Each other should be good enough."

"So why are you marrying me again?" Ronnie asked.

"I have no idea," Elisha said. "It's all about the wedding cake."

"That's the nicest thing you've ever said to me."

Then he did kiss her.

About the Author

Robert Downs aspired to be a writer before he realized how difficult the writing process was. Fortunately, he'd already fallen in love with the craft, otherwise his tales might never have seen print. Originally from West Virginia, he has lived in Virginia, Massachusetts, New Mexico, and now resides in California. When he's not writing, Downs can be found reading, watching movies, traveling, or smiling. To find out more about his latest projects, or to reach out to him on the Internet, visit the author's website: www.RobertDowns.net.